The Christmas Letters

Also by Lee Smith

NOVELS

SHORT STORIES

Praise for *The Christmas Letters:*

"Bless Lee Smith's heart! Once again, the novelist from Chapel Hill, N.C., has proved that nobody knows Southern women better. Once again, her prose is apparently effortless. . . . Once again, she has crafted a sparkling little gem of a story brimming with wit, charm, heartbreak, and even, this time, recipes." —*Chicago Tribune*

"One of our most accomplished authors scores again. . . . joys, tragedies, recipes, and reflections make an affecting narrative that ends much too soon. Highly recommended." —*Library Journal*

"All the gladness and sadness of life are found in this compact volume. . . . [*The Christmas Letters*] reminds us how often the ties that bind can stretch to the breaking point and that there's no better time than Christmas to mend the fraying seams."
—*Southern Living*

"A poignant story of public and private courage, ordinary hardship, and fragile hope; but mostly, it is a story of love."
—*Country Living*

"You will devour this collection." —*Booklist*

"A perfect heart warmer for chilly winter days and a fun stocking stuffer." —*Woman's Day*

"With her typical easy wit and down-home charm, Smith fashions an epistolary novella from that most infamous of genres, the annual family letter that often arrives in Christmas cards. . . . A delight." —*Kirkus Reviews*

"If there's a better Southern writer writing now than Lee Smith, I don't know who it is."
—*The Southern Pines (North Carolina) Pilot*

The Christmas Letters

A Novella by

LEE SMITH

Algonquin Books of Chapel Hill   2002

Published by
ALGONQUIN BOOKS OF CHAPEL HILL
Post Office Box 2225
Chapel Hill, North Carolina 27515-2225

a division of
WORKMAN PUBLISHING
708 Broadway
New York, New York 10003

This is a work of fiction. All names, characters, places, and incidents
are either products of the author's imagination or are used fictitiously.
No reference to any real person is intended or should be inferred.

This novella is based on a short story with the same title that appeared
in the December 1995 issue of *Redbook* magazine.

LIBRARY OF CONGRESS CATALOGING-IN-PUBLICATION DATA
Smith, Lee, 1944–
    The Christmas letters : a novella / Lee Smith.
        p.   cm.
    ISBN 1-56512-156-2
    I. Title.
    PS3569.M5376C48   1996
    813'.54—dc20   96-16116
                                         CIP

ISBN 1-56512-376-X paper

10   9   8   7   6   5   4   3   2

For my family

The Christmas Letters

1. Letters from Birdie

The Christmas Letters

Dec. 24, 1944

Dear Mama and Rachel,

It is the day before Christmas and though I know I should be so happy with my own sweet angel baby Mary who lies right here beside me as I write this letter, I will tell you the truth. I am weepy, and cannot hold back my tears. Why do you reckon this is so, when Mary and me have everything we need here?

Why, we have got a room of our very own nestled up under the eaves of Bill's parents' house, it is a nice little room too, with a low roof that slopes up to a point at the top and the prettiest wallpaper featuring a trellis design covered all over in the most beautiful morning glories you can possibly imagine. They are a deep purply blue, and the trellis is white, it is lovely beyond belief. You know I have always been partial to morning glories. Also in this room there is a big iron bed painted white, a rocking chair, a night table with a funny green lamp that has a yellow lampshade with ball fringe all around it, and a little home-made desk where I now sit to write you this letter. There is also a washstand with a Blue Willow pitcher and bowl and an old black-painted trunk where I can lay my Mary down when I change her diapers. She has a little bassinet as well,

very old, it has been in Bill's family for years and years
though nobody knows where it came from.

So Mary and I are well equipped, and should not want
for a thing in the new year of our Lord 1945, not a thing in
the world except to come back to West Virginia, which we
cannot do.

It is so different here, all flat brown fields which stretch
out from this farmhouse in three directions as far as the eye
can see. But in the fourth direction, South—now this is the
view from our little round window—there is the wide dark
Neuse River moving slowly and mysteriously toward the
Ocean which I have not yet seen and can scarcely imagine
though Bill has promised to take us when he comes home.
And way across the river, there's the town. I can see it better at night when its lights make a pretty reflection in the
water, like jewels. In fact the name of the movie theater in
town is the Bijou which means jewel if I am correct. It is the
colored lights of the Bijou which twinkle in the water come
dark, how I love to look at them.

Still I wish I could have come back up home to have
my baby, and stayed with you all until Bill gets out of the
War, but he would not hear a word about it, not a word,
saying that "No," his own parents would take good care of
his wife and baby. Well, it is the other way around, if you
ask me, since Bill's mother is sick so much. Mrs. Pickett is a
woman who was beautiful once upon a time, I know it is

true for I have seen the pictures. I need to remember that she got spoiled because she was the only child of wealthy parents, and had her way in everything, that this was her parents' house and farm which Bill's father is fast running into the ground, according to all. Come to mention it, I'm finding out that Mr. Slone Pickett has got a reputation around here as a lifelong ne'er-do-well, and a gambler and drunkard besides.

I must say that Bill did not breathe a word of all this to me, and in fact I wonder if he even knows the extent of his father's Reputation. But it may have been that Mr. Pickett minded his P's and Q's better when Dennis and Bill were here working with him, and has only hit this new low since their departure for the War.

I hasten to add that Mr. Pickett does not bother *me* in any way, in fact he is charming to a fault, and seems devoted to little Mary. He likes to bounce her on his knee and sing aloud, "This is the way the Lady rides," etc. But he is seldom here, always gone off "seeing to business," as he puts it, which means sitting around with the other old fellows at Bryce's Tavern across the river, playing cards and talking, or out in his car visiting people. Mr. Pickett loves to go visiting, and I must say I cannot blame him too much, as Mrs. Pickett is not very good company. But this leaves it all up to me, for Mrs. Pickett is quite demanding and it takes both me and old Lorene working double-time just to pacify her.

Mostly she lies in bed reading magazines and romance novels, with her teeth took out and laid on the bedside table. First she wants one thing then another. She eats about 8 little meals every day instead of 3 like normal people, because of an ulcer, she says, and everything has to be just so. For instance you have to cut all the crusts off the bread or she will not eat it.

I don't think I've ever described Bill's parents to you. In appearance Mrs. P. is tall and thin with arms and legs like pipe cleaners, an unusually large head, big blue eyes, and skin so white it looks like milkglass. By contrast, Mr. Pickett is still a handsome man, with thick white hair and eyebrows, though his belly hangs over his belt making him look a little like Humpty Dumpty. He dresses up every day fit to kill, he is quite the dandy. He would *die* if he knew he looks like Humpty Dumpty.

I must say it is a surprise to me that my Bill ever issued forth from this unlikely Union, as Bill is such a plain and straightforward fellow, so likable and easy-going, or so it seems to me, though I swear I have nearly forgot his face now as he has been gone already for longer than I knew him before the War.

I have thought and thought about that day we met, until I wonder if I really remember it at all, or if it is merely a story I made up and now play again and again in my mind like a movie over at the Bijou. I don't know if I have told you all the particulars of it or not, but I would like to, and I hope you will not mind me going on at length, for I miss you so much, and love to think of you reading this long letter from me.

You remember that I had come down to North Carolina on that trip with Adelaide Harper to visit her Aunt and Uncle who planned to travel down the Neuse for five days on their new houseboat, and Adelaide was to come with them, as the trip would be Educational. Remember how much I loved Adelaide, Mama, and how I begged to come? Do you ever wish you had said "No," I wonder now, and do you ever think about where I might be instead, and what I might be doing? Instead of nursing a baby, I mean, on a lonely farm in the middle of brown fields gone to seed down here in North Carolina? For I do wonder about these things. I have time now to wonder, and think on everything, and I find myself thinking, "Oh, but if—" or "If only—" as it has struck me that our whole lives may be so determined, in the twinkling of an eye. Oh but I cannot imagine my life if I had never met Bill at all, this is the Truth.

I will never forget the day the houseboat ran against the bridge, that sudden awful Storm, almost a hurricane they said it was, and we were forced to seek shelter in the empty barn not a mile from where I now sit to write you this letter, and before we could properly get our wits about us, here came Bill to save us and bring us home. I remember that it was almost dark and we were so scared, Adelaide and me all hugged up together as tight as you please and crying to beat the band, when Bill appeared in the barn door with a smile as bright as the lantern he held in his hands.

"Now, girls, it can't be all that bad!" he said. "Isn't that right, Ma'am?" Now he was addressing Adelaide's Aunt. "For here you are, safe and sound after all, and the storm has passed, and you're to come along home with me and get some supper and dry your clothes."

And so we followed him out across the great dark flooded fields, sinking to our ankles in water, which mattered not a whit at that point as we were soaked through and through already. Bill talked to Adelaide's Uncle on the way, telling all the particulars of the Storm and the havoc it had wrought all up and down the river, while Adelaide and I held hands and strained to see Bill's shape in the gloom ahead. I have to say, I was pretty much taken with Bill from the get-go, as you used to say, Mama. Still, I thought that if he were to take notice of either of us, it would be Adelaide of course, for she was the pretty one with the curly blond ringlets admired by all.

When we finally got to Bill's house, it quickly became apparent that his grand invitation was ill-considered, for there sat his Mother wrapped up in a shawl by a sputtering oil lamp, and no supper either visible or forthcoming. I saw the situation and took charge, since Adelaide's Aunt had to go lie down immediately and Adelaide herself did not know how to do anything of that nature. And you know how I have always loved to cook.

"Do you have any cornmeal?" I asked Bill's mother, who had not the foggiest notion.

But Bill found the cornmeal for me, and some Bourbon Whiskey for Adelaide's Uncle, and then the lights came back on and I set to work in earnest, wearing by now an old flannel nightshirt belonging to Bill's Father, and going barefoot in the kitchen. By and by Adelaide and her Aunt reappeared, wearing some of Mrs. Pickett's clothes, and her Uncle cheered up under the influence of the Whiskey, and the whole evening began to take on a festive aspect. As for myself, I could scarcely cook, for I kept stealing glances at Bill.

"Ah, now he will fall in love with Adelaide," I thought, when they two fell into conversation, for he had not said one word directly to me. Anyway I boiled potatoes and fried up some corn dodgers the way you taught me, Mama, and then I asked for ham and was told to go down to the cellar to get it, and did, still barefooted. I recall how cool and damp the bricks felt to my feet. But what a surprise when I turned around to find Bill right there, right behind me, he had followed without a word.

"Now what is your name again?" he asked without

preamble and I said, "Mary Bird Hodges," though I scarce could talk, and he said, "And are you spoken for?" and I said, "No," forgetting all about William Isley in that instant, and Bill said, "Well, then," and picked me up and kissed me hard, and I saw Stars, I swear I did, before my very eyes, and could not breathe when he set me back down. Then all of a sudden we fell to laughing, we were *both* of us laughing like crazy, for no reason at all, and on and on until we had to sit down on the floor, we were so out of breath. Then Bill leaned over and kissed me again, just a little kiss, and by the time we had got ourselves back together and gone upstairs with the ham, we had an understanding, or I *felt* we had an understanding, and both Adelaide and her Aunt later said it was plain to them as well, that we were glowing, and apt to break into giggles when nothing was funny that anyone else could see.

So this is the exact circumstances of how we met, which I take great pleasure in remembering over and over alone in my little room with my little Mary, and in writing to you. For it is my fondest hope, Rachel, that you will one day meet a man as fine as Bill, and fall in love as I have done.

You know the rest, how he came up home to call on us, and stayed a week, and then came back and talked me into eloping, which I know you have never forgiven me for yet, Mama, I reckon I cannot blame you. But I *had* to have Bill, that was all there was to it. And there was problems with

The Christmas Letters

Mr. and Mrs. Pickett, Bill did not say what at the time, but now I see that she would have opposed the match, thinking nobody in this world is good enough for her or hers. Well, be that as it may, I could not have done otherwise. I would have followed Bill anywhere on the earth. I hope you have come to understand this, and are thinking about me more kindly than at first. This course has not been altogether easy for me either, as I am trying to tell you. It is not a bed of roses by any means.

And now I fear that this farm is teetering right on the edge of Ruin, though no one has discussed it with me of course, nor will they. But Mr. Pickett is evading certain creditors, of this I am sure. With Dennis God knows where in the Pacific and my own poor Bill off in New Guinea, both so far away.

Oh, who can know the Future? Who would have ever thought to find me here, or my best friend Adelaide dead of pneumonia, all these long months? It breaks my heart to think of Adelaide, as it breaks my heart to think of the mountains, and all of you.

I just know that Granddaddy will shoot off the gun on Christmas morning, that you will cook a hen for dinner, Mama, Daddy will make the eggnog, and Great-Aunt Lydia will give everybody those awful-looking crocheted placemats again that she has been making for years and years. It makes me laugh to think about them! I send a special hug to the little Twins, and love to Daddy, and to everybody. I trust you are all well, and have a fine holiday, and that you miss me too, at least a little, and think about me down here in North Carolina so far from home. Oh, now I am crying again. But I have made my bed and I will lie in it the way I was taught, you may rest assured of that. I will do you proud.

Bill writes that it is real hot in New Guinea, and that he has bought some little carved wooden animals from the Natives, for our Mary, and that he loves me. I know this is true, though it fills me with fear too, for Bill does not *really* know me, nor I him. Sometimes I wonder if it is possible for *any* person to know any other, I mean to *really* know them? Often I sit in this rocking chair by my little round window nursing Mary and looking out across the big slow river at the lights of town twinkling so far away, and I feel lonesome beyond words. But I will put my faith in God and trust him to take good care of me and my baby while we all wait for sweet Bill to come home.

> *So, Happy New Year 1945*
> *From Your Loving,*
> *Birdie*

P.S. This is just about the only thing I can get Mrs. Pickett to eat, so I try to make it as often as I can, in spite of rationing.

BIRDIE'S BOILED CUSTARD

3 eggs	3 cups milk
½ cup sugar	½ teas. vanilla

Beat eggs, add sugar and milk. Cook in double boiler until mixture will coat a spoon. Add vanilla when cool.

Dec. 22, 1951

Dear Mama and Rachel,

First, good luck on Robert Tipping, Rachel! He sounds perfect, though I should think it would be a big responsibility to be a minister's wife. Both of you, please keep me posted. I promise that I will be a better correspondent than I have been lately. My excuse is that I have been saving up my thoughts and news for this annual Christmas Letter, though it is worth my life to write it, as baby Ruthie is *already walking* and into everything, she leads me a merry chase! My little Mary is still as good as gold, however, playing nonstop with her brother Joe, they are not a bit of trouble but rather a blessing to me. It may be because they are scarcely two years apart in age—Joe was *Unexpected*, shall we say—that they are so close in temperament as well, act-ing more like Twins than like Brother and Sister. Mary has always been a serious child. I think the circumstances of her birth, plus all that time alone with me when I was so homesick in the beginning, have made her grave beyond her years. And then her daddy's homecoming was bittersweet at best, with the whole family mourning Dennis, so recently fallen at Corregidor. Mary never saw her Uncle Dennis, but she took all these events to heart, I believe, the way children will—for children *do* know everything happening in a household, whether anyone tells them or not.

But Joe's birth brought Mary back out into the sunshine, affording her the greatest Joy. She did everything for him from the first, and as he's grown, you cannot pry them apart. Everybody has marveled at it, the sweetness of brother and sister, their grave concern for each other at all times. Why, they even have a little language all their own, which they have had ever since Joe learned to talk, and sometimes they will still fall into it, especially if others are present and they want to speak privately to one another. It used to worry Bill, he is so down-to-earth. But I said, Where is the harm? As long as they are capable of speaking plain English when they need to?

And they *are* capable, they are smart as a whip, both of them, and doing fine in school. While at home they race through their chores in order to have more time for these endless games of "Pretend" which they never tire of, games which come right out of their heads, where they are knights and ladies or Robin Hood or saints of old or the Hardy Boys or whatever. I swear, you can't tell *what* they will come up with!

Ruthie by contrast is not reflective at all but very Active, she reminds me of a little puppy. I have had to go through the whole living room, putting everything breakable up where she can't reach, something I never worried about with either Mary or Joe.

But concerning children, the big news is that Bill's sister in Richmond has died of a fever and now his nephews are coming to live with us too. Bill invited them for the remainder of the year, he says they can help him farm. I just about died when he told me. For I have not got enough hands as it is, now that Mr. Pickett has disappeared and I am taking care of Bill's mother full-time, and I have to say, she is the most Demanding woman in the world. She just lies in bed wanting first one thing and then another, for instance I have to keep her well supplied with snuff and ice water at all times. Of course Bill takes up for her, saying she is broken-hearted at the death of Dennis, not to mention Mr. Pickett's desertion. Bill believes that his mother really is sick, too, saying that she has "congestive heart failure," which I think she has made up out of whole cloth, having read about it in a magazine. Oh, I know better than to say a word. Though secretly I think she is healthy as a horse, and will outlive us all.

But my Bill is so generous, he does not even have anything bad to say about his *Father*, which astounds me. He says his father had a run of hard luck, that's all, and that Dennis's death pushed him over the edge. I did not mention the grocer's daughter who is rumored to have left town at the same time as Mr. Pickett. When I asked Bill what he would do if Mr. Pickett should just show up on the front porch one day, Sober for a change, and ask to come back home, why Bill said he would *take him in of course*, and chided me for feeling otherwise. "Birdie," he said, "where is all that famous Christian charity I have heard so much about?" Bill was just grinning ear to ear, for he knew he had me there.

My dear Bill remains as good-natured and sweet as ever despite our financial problems. Those clear brown eyes of his are always fixed upon the Future, full of hope. Now he is trying something new, called soybeans. The government is urging everybody to plant them. They are the crop of the future apparently, to be used in a lot of different ways, though they are not a bit good to cook with, tasting awful.

By the way we sent you a tin of peanuts on the train, I hope you got them in time for Christmas. It still never really seems like Christmas to me down here, even now, for it scarcely snows and of course I never get over missing the mountains. Yet I hasten to say I am a Happy Woman, for the longer I live with Bill, the more I love and respect him, as he is a truly good man. He would give anybody the very shirt off his back, he is famous for it.

And Bill is *fun*, too, I hasten to add, for pure goodness can wear on a person over time. Why, just the other night, for instance, he came in and slipped up on me from behind, and kissed my ear and untied my apron, and announced that we were going dancing.

"Dancing!" I said. "Why, where will we do that?" for there is no place around here to dance.

"Right here," Bill said with a whoop, "at Uncle Bill's Hot Spot," and then he produced the Christmas gift which he had bought for me in town that day, a beautiful brand new Philco Radio. He just couldn't wait until Christmas to give it to me! He plugged it in and turned it on, and soon the kitchen was filled with the lively music of Benny Goodman. Bill twirled me around and then we were jitterbugging like crazy, you know that both of us are real good dancers. After that came another tune, and then another. We danced on and on as the children crept into the kitchen one after another, Mary and Joe holding hands, while all the water boiled out of my potatoes and they burned up, I even had to throw away the pan. "Never mind!" Bill said, putting on my apron himself to cook us a big breakfast, bacon and eggs being the only food he knows how to cook. "Go on, honey!" he said to me. "Go take a nice long bath, I'll call you when breakfast is ready."

"Breakfast!" Mrs. Pickett fluttered into the kitchen like a little old moth, clinging to the cabinets. "Why, what in the world! Birdie, where do you think you're going?" The last thing I saw was her scandalized old face as I headed off down the hall to draw up a deep bath, where I had a good laugh all by myself, in a ton of bubbles.

So you see that Bill has not been beat down yet by all our misfortunes with the farm, and remains near Perfect in my eyes. I just wish he would come to church with me but I can't get him to, at least not *yet*. So I take my precious children, and pray for us all, and remain

> *Your loving,*
> *Birdie*

P.S. Mama, it's fine with me that you pass my Christmas letters around if you want to. And since I know you are expecting another recipe from me, here it is, courtesy of Mrs. Eugenia Goodwillie at church, who is fat as can be, and always wears this bright green hat. I wish you could see her! Anyway, here goes—we have got a real tradition now, haven't we?

The Christmas Letters

MRS. GOODWILLIE'S BIBLE CAKE

1 cup butter (Judges 5:25)
3½ cups flour (I Kings 4:22)
3 cups sugar (Jeremiah 6:20)
2 cups raisins (I Samuel 30:12)
2 cups figs (I Samuel 30:12)
1 cup water (Genesis 24:17)
1 cup almonds (Genesis 43:11)
6 eggs (Isaiah 10:14)
1 tsp. honey (Exodus 16:31)
pinch of salt (Leviticus 2:13)
2 tsp. baking powder (I Corinthians 5:6)
spice to taste (I Kings 10:10)

Follow Solomon's advice for making good
boys and girls and you will have a good cake
(Proverbs 23:14).

Christmas 1956

*To Mama and Daddy, Rachel and Robert,
and Other Dear Family and Friends,*
    I know you will excuse the lack of a Christmas letter

from me last year, when you hear what we have been through, and do we ever have some Big News for you!

I was just thinking how God never sends us more than we can bear, and how what appears as Calamity can often be a blessing in disguise.

First, the Calamity of spring before last—which you know about already, but I want to tell you just how it was when it happened, so you will know how we felt at the time, and what it is like to be in a Flood. The first thing is, it does not happen all at once. It takes days. Days and days and days of too much rain, it is just a conversation piece for a while, as in, "Have you ever seen so much rain?" But then—and you are not sure exactly when this starts to happen—you start feeling Blue, as there is never much sun to be seen, and the children start to get on your nerves. And then there comes the time that all conversation ceases whenever the rain starts up again on the old tin roof, and Bill puts down his newspaper, and stands, and starts to pace back and forth in the hall.

There are respites, of course. A morning, an afternoon of no rain for a change, when the men walk down to the end of the road and stand on the bank smoking cigarettes and looking out over the river, and nobody's talking. By then the crops have been flooded out once, and it's too wet to plant again. And it just *keeps on raining*, a light sprinkle, then a downpour, then a quick gusty shower, then another sprinkle. . . . But it never stops, not really, and this goes on for a month. On flat land, a Flood is a long time coming.

And in the meantime, everything changes. The river goes from being merely the distant scenic backdrop of the landscape to become an awful Force in and of itself, still slow but growing in speed and power every day, inching up its banks, with brown churning eddies and whirlpools and currents now in its broad expanse, so that to stand and watch it is to watch some huge and strong and ever-changing Monster come slowly to life. The willows on the banks stand half-submerged, trailing their branches forlornly downstream. One day the old boat shed that stood at the end of the road is gone, simply gone, and then the end of the road is gone too. Now we sit on chairs in the yard to watch the river, and now it is almost like a movie, something different every few minutes, as somebody's doghouse floats past, then a washtub, a chair, logs and debris, a roof, a man's straw hat, a rocking horse.

Word comes from everywhere: the bridge is out at Barberville, they are sandbagging at Duncan, they are already evacuating Little Point, downriver. We are glued to the radio. I start collecting rainwater. In the gathering excitement, the children run wild. And more news comes: they are evacuating Powell's Neck, old man Burgess won't leave, they tie him up and carry him out on a stretcher, his daughter has signed a paper. Miss Treadway, the piano teacher, is in hysterics, they have taken her to the Hospital.

Bill's mother remains surprisingly calm in the face of this Disaster, in fact it comes to me that she is actually *enjoying* all the excitement. Her eyes glow like lamps in her yellow face and she never leaves the porch where she sits in state on the glider, wrapped up in blankets and wearing her Sunday hat, chatting with all who come by. For the first time ever, Bill is short with her, cutting her off in mid-sentence as she rambles on and on.

Not only that, but he *spanks* Ruthie—something he has never done before.

Of course Ruthie *did* scare us all to death by disappearing like that, gone for over two hours without thinking to tell any of us that she was going to see her little friend, whose parents had picked her up in a car and taken her home for a visit. We were frantic. Bill paddled her good, until *everybody* was crying, Joe above all, pulling at his daddy until Bill smacked him too, causing Joe to disappear for the rest of the afternoon. Bill was not himself. He seemed exhausted when it was over, a man in a daze. He went upstairs and lay down on our bed like a Corpse in a coffin, very stiff, with his hands folded up on his chest. I did not dare to mention the mud on the quilt, I believe we both knew by then that it would not matter. I tiptoed over to kiss my Bill but his face was Stone, and he lay exactly like that until the sheriff came to the door a few hours later and said that we would have to leave.

In a way, this was a relief. Bill got up. The children suddenly turned into little Angels, very helpful, and we all worked with a common purpose, loading up the car and truck, carrying everything else upstairs. We packed the attic full, and that room up under the eaves where I had stayed with my little Mary so long ago.

One of the last things I did before we left was to look out my little round window again, at a whole world gone wild, the mysterious dark river that I had loved, which had held so much promise somehow, now turned against us— wide, yellow, and Evil, rising every hour up the long green bank with its edging of lacy froth. The sun was out by the time we left, but it made no difference, of course, as the river was on the rise.

I couldn't believe it—suddenly, it had turned into the prettiest afternoon. Joe and Mary whispered to each other all the way to Cartersville, playing their games, off in their own little world, and I was just as glad of it, for the Real World seemed too harsh that day for children, and I knew I was powerless to protect them, or any of us, from it.

For the first time in my life, I questioned God's wisdom and His will, for I had prayed to Him all along, and yet He had done nothing, and had allowed this to happen to us. I was full of bitterness, and the bright sunshiny day only seemed to make it worse in my estimation, as if He was mocking me. We took shelter at the Presbyterian Church in Pasquotank, which was far enough inland to be judged safe. There we found sandwiches and coffee, and other children for our children to play with, and I must say that Bill's mother seemed to enjoy the whole experience enormously.

I did not. My mind was filled with what must be happening back at home, and I remained cut off from my beloved husband, as from God. Bill went back out directly in the truck with the other men, and came back in the late afternoon with a set gray face. "It is over, Birdie," he said, and turned away, but then in the night on the hard church floor, he broke and started crying and so was restored to me, and I thanked God, though I knew we had lost the farm.

One of the worst things about a flood is that—unlike a fire, which makes a clean sweep of everything—when the waters recede at last, everything is unfortunately *Still There*, and though it is all ruined beyond hope, there it yet is, to be dealt with. You feel like you *ought* to clean things up, you *ought* to be able to use them again, but the truth is, you cannot.

We had to walk across the muddy fields to our house, for the road was gone, and pull ourselves up through the open door, for the porch was gone. Inside we found a foot of stinking mud throughout the entire first story, and the biggest ugliest Catfish I have ever seen was flopping around on the kitchen floor. At that point, I just sat down in the mud and cried my eyes out. After all the work we— especially Bill—had put into that sorry farm, it broke my heart! At that point Joe caught the Catfish with his bare hands, and Bill killed it with a knife, and they carried it in a croker sack over to the church ladies, who put it in a big pot of chowder which they were making at the church. I couldn't eat a bite of supper, I couldn't get the awful picture out of my mind, how it looked as it flopped in the mud on my kitchen floor, with its awful grinning face, its wide smart eyes, those sweeping whiskers, oh I would have nightmares about that Catfish for months to come.

Well, to make a long story short, we lost the farm.

But I have to say, if it hadn't happened, why, we would be out there still, I reckon, both of us, working our fingers to the bone every day, just trying to make ends meet. Bill would never have got up the nerve to get that bank loan and start the dime store. For Necessity truly *is* the Mother of Invention, as they say.

So now, here we are living in town, on the other side of that river which has receded of course and now flows within its banks as pretty as you please.

And our dime store is a real big Success! As some of you have heard from me already. Everybody comes to shop, as there is nothing like it for miles around. Bill sells everything you can think of, from nails to sheets to makeup. We've even got a popcorn machine! And a candy counter with candy corn, fudge, jellied orange slices, non-pareils, why you name it.

And I am the proud proprietor of Birdie's Lunch, which we have built into one corner of the store. You know how much I have always loved to cook. Well, Birdie's Lunch is very popular, I have to say. I am open for Breakfast and Lunch only, though some people buy their Supper and carry it home, especially on chicken and dumpling days. My meatloaf is another very popular item. Best of all is, I get to see Bill all day long, not only at supper time, when he is dog tired, as on the farm. And all the children work at the store with us, they all have jobs, and are a big help.

Last year at Eastertime, we had them all helping us to make Easter baskets. It took me and Bill and everybody else that works for us, plus the kids, we had formed a regular little Assembly Line. This was on a Sunday afternoon after church when the store was closed, several weeks before Easter. It was a cool rainy day as I recall, and I had made some coffee and chocolate chip and oatmeal cookies to give everybody, so we had kind of a Party Atmosphere, and we were all enjoying ourselves. We had boxes of Easter candy and little toy rabbits and bunnies and such as that, yellow and purple cellophane paper which came in long rolls, and several huge cardboard boxes filled with pink cellophane Easter straw. I was the one who tied the bows, I have always been very good at bows. We worked all afternoon. I was so busy, and having such a good time, that I didn't even notice when Mary and Joe disappeared. Then suddenly it was time to go, and we couldn't find them anywhere.

"Mary! Joe!" we called all over the store, and finally here they came, popping right up out of the last box of Easter straw, nearly scaring us all to death! They had crawled down under the straw, and fallen asleep there. Oh how we laughed! We are all enjoying the dime store.

Mary comes down to the store every day after school. From the very beginning, she has always "taken care of the dolls" for Bill, dusting them and fixing their hair, arranging them on the shelf. She makes up names for them, and a life story for each one. Sometimes I swear I don't know what will become of our Mary, she is *too smart* for a little girl. I fear that she may have trouble adjusting to the world because of it. She is certainly "our little scholar," making straight A's in school. Why, Mary would rather read than eat! This is absolutely true.

Meanwhile Ruthie can scarcely sit still long enough to get her homework. She is crazy about Acrobatics and Tap Dancing, which she takes from a Miss Lovett who comes over from Goodlettsville and holds classes at the American Legion twice a week. There are many more opportunities here in town, which we are taking full advantage of.

Joe is a Boy Scout, for instance, he is so good with his

hands and can make anything. Joe puts together the air-
plane and automobile models for display in the dime store,
and sweeps the floor, and Bill pays him.

More than anything, Bill and I want these children to
have the opportunity to go to college, which we never had.
So we are all working together, and though the hours are
long and sometimes it seems that we will *never* get this loan
paid off, still we are all together, and the future looks bright
to me as I see that God had a greater good in mind than we
could envision when he sent us that flood, which is why I
said at the beginning of this long letter, Calamity can often
be a Blessing in Disguise.

Even old Mrs. Pickett likes our new life. Her personality
is much improved. Bill has bought her a hearing aid and a
new set of teeth, which make her look exactly like a horse, I
have to say, but she sits now on a lawn chair in the front of
the dime store talking to everybody, and everybody is amazed
by how old she is, and how much she has got to say. Of
course, I am not amazed, and I am glad she chooses to place
her lawn chair by the Checkout instead of my lunch counter.

> *Lots of love and a very
> merry Christmas 1956
> from your busy, busy, busy
> Birdie*

P.S. Kids love these. They are good for Christmas giving, too, as they will keep in a tin for ages. I have made a ton of them this Christmas season.

STICKS AND STONES

½ cup butter or margarine, melted
4½ teaspoons Worcestershire sauce
1½ teas. salt
8 cups cereal (Cheerios and Chex)
1 cup nuts
1 cup pretzels

Mix well, bake 1 hour at 250°, stirring every 15 minutes.

Christmas 1962

Dear All,

If I thought I was busy before, I have to say, it is nothing compared to now, what with Mary and Joe in High School, and going off like firecrackers in every direction. I swear, there is so much for kids to do these days! I think it is wonderful. It is surely not a bit like when we were growing up in Blue Gap, and had to work so hard, and then find amusement among ourselves. I can still remember how much I hated to hoe that corn, and how that old burley tobacco would stick to your arms and hands. Those were hard times, I reckon, but they seem sweet to me now, and almost golden somehow, as seen through the haze of the years. Don't you recall how we all used to sit out on the porch of an evening, and talk? Why, we would talk about everything, I reckon we didn't have anything else to do, but my, those were some good stories we heard, weren't they? Don't you remember Granddaddy telling about the Ghost Dog? And old Aunt Lydia was so funny, without even knowing it. Don't you remember that story she used to tell about the time when she was coming out of church and some woman behind her, I believe it was old Mrs. Greenleaf, said to her, "Why, Lydia, I'll swear, honey, you look so pretty from the back!" Don't you remember Lydia telling that, and then saying, "Now, girls, I don't know whether I ought to get mad or not!" and asking all us little girls what we thought about it. We got so tickled at her, well it's all so long ago, isn't it? It was a Different World.

And nobody ever sits on the front porch here even though we have got one. We are all too busy, it seems, what with me and Bill down at the dime store all the time, and the kids in and out so fast, so busy with all their activities.

When I think of our own front porch now, I think of the screen door slamming all day long. "Don't slam the door!" I used to call out, "Don't slam the door!" but now I scarcely bother. It is the pace of Modern Life which has made all the difference, even down here in such a pokey little town as ours. And if anybody today has a moment to sit, they are likely to sit in front of the television, which *is* wonderful, I have to say, you can always find something to be interested in. Mrs. Pickett has to watch her "story," as she calls it, every afternoon, this being "Search for Tomorrow." "Isn't that Andrea Whiting just *awful*?" Mrs. Pickett will ask everybody, but she wouldn't miss a day if it killed her.

The kids are fine, though Joe has gotten in a scrape or two, boys will be boys, I reckon. He is just crazy about a car, any car, and I must say that Bill aids and abets him in this pastime, having bought him three to date, which they are always "working on." Joe is just as likely to be found *under* a car as driving it, and though I may complain about his dirty clothes and mediocre school reports, this is clearly his passion, and his talent.

I guess it will remain up to Mary to be my scholar, and in fact it looks as though she will be the Valedictorian of her class this June if she can keep her grades up. Or she may end up in a tie with Ernest Birdsong (a Brain). We are very proud of Mary who was awarded the Rotary Club Scholarship at a lovely Semi-formal Dinner in November, to be applied toward the college of her choice. She has applied to several schools, all of them fairly near by, as Bill says he could not stand for her to go *too* far from home. Her first choice is the Woman's College in Greensboro, but we hope she will go to Longwood which is also a teachers' college, and closer to us. Mary says she is going to be an English teacher. She idolizes Mrs. Diane Hope, her senior English teacher, who graduated from W.C. herself. (This is the big appeal of Greensboro.)

Mary also takes after me in liking to cook, in fact she won the 4-H Cooking Contest last spring with her Carrot Cake recipe, and would have won the Regional except that she forgot to wear a hairnet at the competition, I think this is so silly.

I have always privately hoped that Mary would make the most of her God-given writing talent, for she has been writing poems and stories ever since she was a little child. No one in this neighborhood will ever forget *The Small Review*, Mary's newspaper, which she wrote all by herself and then got Joe to help her copy out by hand, and sell it door to door. Some of the news items were so funny, such as "Miss Mary Pickett and Miss Ruthie Pickett were taken on a shopping trip to Raleigh by their mother, Mrs. William Pickett of 110 Maple Avenue. They bought new shoes at Buster Brown and enjoyed the opportunity to look at the bones of their feet through a machine. Their bones are green." How we all laughed at that! But I had to make Mary apologize to our neighbor across the street for her editorial, "Mr. George Maguire Is Too Grumpy." And once when we had taken the children to the Outer Banks for a vacation, Bill found a beautiful Poem that Mary had written and then crumpled up and left in a dresser drawer, entitled "The Merry-Go-Round of Life." It was just beautiful, and impossible to believe it had been written by a twelve-year-old girl, which Mary was at the time. Bill folded it up and put it in his billfold, he has carried it around ever since. Sometimes he will take it out and read it aloud to somebody, if the occasion arises, which just embarrasses Mary to death. You know how teenagers are! So, I harbor some hopes that my Mary will be a writer, but you may rest assured that we will be proud of her whatever she does.

And as for Ruthie, it is becoming clear that she might do just about anything. Bill has always said, "Ruthie is a firecracker!" This fall she was a J.V. Football Cheerleader, you ought to see her turning cartwheels out across the field. Now she is practicing for the Miss Elementary School Pageant, she is driving us all crazy by singing "I Enjoy Being a Girl" over and over, which will be her Talent. Since Mary and Joe were going to Myrtle Beach with the youth group from church last summer, I felt I should go as one of

the chaperones, which I did, and it was a lot of fun but No
Vacation, I have to say.

> *Merry Christmas from all
> the Picketts,
> Mary, Joe, Ruthie, Birdie
> and Bill*

P.S. Here is Mary's prize-winning recipe for Carrot Cake.
Be sure to wear a hairnet (ha ha).

MARY'S CARROT CAKE

2 cups sifted flour	1 cup salad oil
2 teaspoons baking powder	4 eggs
1½ teas. baking soda	2 cups finely grated carrots
2 teas. cinnamon	1 8½ oz. can flaked coconut
1½ teas. salt	½ c. chopped nuts
2 cups sugar	

Preheat oven to 350°. Sift together flour, baking
powder, baking soda, salt, and cinnamon. Add
sugar, oil, and eggs; beat well. Add carrots, nuts,
and coconut; blend thoroughly. Pour into 3
9-inch round layer-cake pans that have been
greased and floured. Bake in moderate oven 35 to
40 minutes. Remove from oven, cool a few minutes

in pans. Turn out on wire racks and cool thoroughly. Fill layers, and frost top and sides of cake with cream cheese frosting.

CREAM CHEESE FROSTING

> ½ cup butter
> 1 8-oz. package cream cheese
> 1 teas. vanilla
> 1 lb. confectioner's sugar

Combine butter, cream cheese, and vanilla; cream well. Beat sugar in, adding milk if necessary.

Dec. 24, 1966

Dearest Family,

I apologize for these carbon copies, I hope you can read them. Too bad Mary and Joe are all grown up now and can't copy this letter out for me, as they did in their *Small Review*, so long ago. But I am in a hurry, and we have a *lot* of news.

Our lovely Mary is now Mrs. Sandy Copeland, having Eloped in a romantic trip to South Carolina in the dead of night. Sandy is a carpenter and such a nice young man, we love him like a son already. Sandy and Mary met in the drugstore in Farmville, Virginia, where Mary was enrolled at Longwood College prior to her marriage. Naturally we were disappointed when she dropped out of school, but as Mary says, "Mom, I can finish school *anytime*." Of course this is true. Bill and I are not too old to remember those early Days of Romance ourselves. After a very brief wedding trip (apparently it is easier to get married in South Carolina), they are living in Petersburg, Virginia, where Sandy works. Mary is not crazy about Petersburg, but she says she will be happy anywhere as long as she is with Sandy.

The other big news is, Joe is now in the Army serving Uncle Sam. We all went through much soul-searching before he left, I have to say. I will not even go into the endless discussions that took place night after night around our kitchen table after dinner, with Joe voicing all his objections to War in general and this War in particular, and Bill trying to tell him what is Right, and urging him not to make a decision that would ruin his life forever. This long discussion was cut short when Joe was drafted, and in the twinkling of an eye, he was gone. Now he is in Bien Hoa. I have worried and worried over it myself, and wish that the Lord would provide us with easier answers. Bill has put a big map of southeast Asia on the wall so he can see where Joe is at all times.

Speaking of Bill, his Health is still not too good though

he continues to go down to the store every day without fail, I don't know what he would do with himself if this was not the case. He will be having some more tests at the University Hospital in early January, maybe they can find out what is wrong. As Bill says, his get-up-and-go has got up and went!

Speaking of get-up-and-go, Ruthie says she is going to major in Business when she goes to college, now who would ever have thought it? She was our light-hearted child. I will never forget that comedy routine she did at the March of Dimes benefit, dressed as a Bum.

In closing, I ask you to remember both Joe and Bill in your prayers, and ask God to bless our Country, and our boys in uniform.

Christmas Blessings from
Birdie and Bill

P.S. We are going to be *grandparents*! I can't wait! I believe I am just as excited as Mary and Sandy are.

P.P.S. And even a sick man can't resist:

BILL'S FAVORITE FUDGE

1 12-oz. package chocolate chips
4 c. miniature marshmallows
1 c. peanut butter

Melt peanut butter and chocolate chips over low
heat until smooth. Gradually stir in marshmallows.
Pour into 9-inch square pan and chill until firm.
Cut into squares.

Dec. 18, 1967

To my dear Family,

I want to begin this Christmas letter by remembering
Bill. You know that he died In Peace on August 10, at home,
with me beside him, as I have been through Life. I woke up
at the crack of dawn that morning, it was a Tuesday, filled
with the strangest sense of deep peace yet a terrible urgency
at the same time, and went immediately to his side.

I had been sleeping for months on a little rollaway cot
right next to Bill's hospital bed which we had put in the living room so everybody could visit him, you know how
much he always loved company. Somehow I was not surprised to find Bill wide awake too, though he had been
sleeping around the clock for several days.

"Hi there, Birdie honey," he said, and I said, "Hi." It
was scarcely light, but I could see him well, his brown eyes
as bright and lively as when we first met, all those years ago.
He grinned at me like the young man he was back then,

a touch of the devil in him, and so I kissed his lips, and squeezed his hand, and sat there with him all day long while he slept as peaceful as a child until the late afternoon when he stirred a bit and then was gone, along with a little breeze that blew through the house just then like an angel passing.

At first I did not see how I could go on alone, but we have to, don't we? We have to do what we have to do, and God will give us the Strength for it, as I have learned, bless His sweet name. And speaking of God, there is one more thing I want to say here and now, since many of you know how mad I used to get at Bill for not going to church. It is this. If there is a heaven, and I believe with all my heart that there is, then my Bill is right there, right now, even though I know he would rather be in the dime store. And I know I will be joining him by and by.

In the meantime, James Grady has taken over the dime store for me. Most of you know James who has worked for Bill since he was a high school boy, he has a Sterling Character. Though I had planned to retire from Birdie's Lunch, nobody will have it, and so I have bowed to Popular Opinion and stayed on. James is putting in some booths, they will be real nice. It will look more like a real restaurant. Also I have a more modern menu now, including taco salads which are a big hit.

I have saved the best part for last.

I am so happy to announce the Birth of my adorable

grandson Andrew Bird Copeland, born June 10 in Rex Hospital, Raleigh, N.C., 7 lb. 8 oz. He came into this world with a full head of black hair to everyone's amazement, you know Mary is so fair. But then the black hair fell out and Mary says it is coming back in blond now, and she further reports that the baby looks more and more like his daddy every day.

Little Andrew is *Just Perfect* in my opinion, of course I am not prejudiced at all!

And I'm just so glad he had a chance to meet Bill.

Joe got to come home for Bill's funeral, he has lost 20 pounds and looks very handsome in his uniform, but he was all upset about his daddy of course, and about what is going on over there as well, though he did not want to talk about it. I guess Joe is just not cut out for war, and often I wonder if we made the right decision in urging him to go.

Bill thought it would make a man of him, but I don't know. I don't know what to think about it. I pray for Joe daily, as for all our boys in this awful and confusing War, and ask you to do the same.

I guess that's about all, except I should add that Mrs. Pickett—still going strong at 100—got a birthday card from Lyndon Johnson.

May God bless each and every one of you this Christmas Season,

Birdie

2. *Letters from Mary*

Dec. 26, 1967

Dear Family,

My apologies for mimeographing this letter to stick in your card, but please consider it a very personal Merry Christmas anyway, from me and Sandy and ANDREW BIRD COPELAND who is six months old at this time, almost completely bald but the cutest baby in the whole world according to his proud parents MR. AND MRS. SANDY COPELAND of #20 Greenacres Park, Raleigh, N.C., where we have now moved as Sandy says there is more opportunity here in the building trades.

Greenacres Park is actually a *trailer park*, and we are living in a rented trailer which would not have been my first choice, as it is aqua, but it *is* very reasonable since *everything* is furnished—wall-to-wall carpet (yuck—more aqua!), blinds and drapes at the windows, a built-in bar and stools in the little kitchen, etc. All this is lucky for us since we have started our housekeeping on a shoestring, you might say. Of course, the size of this trailer *is* a little bit small for Sandy (who is 6'3", after all!). He has to walk around hunched over all the time. But he works so much that he is not home a lot, so it is okay, and will suit us fine until we can afford to move to another place. Actually this

43

trailer reminds me of a dollhouse—remember when I "took care of the dolls" for Daddy? I was so proud of myself. The big difference is, this little doll is *real*!

I wonder if everybody is so crazy about their first baby, and so worried about him. Even though Andy is sleeping through the night now, I still wake up every three hours and can't go back to sleep until I have tiptoed over to his crib just to see if he is still breathing, and I'm happy to report that so far, he *is*! And one *nice* thing about the size of a trailer is that I can check on Andy constantly. We are never far apart in here!

When Sandy comes home from work in the evenings, he always asks me what I've been doing all day, and honestly I don't know how to answer this question. "I can't exactly remember," I tell him, "but whatever it was, it just wore me out!"

The truth is that with a baby, the time flies. Of course I can remember how, as a teenager in the not-so-distant past, I used to get so bored. Sundays, for instance, just dragged on and on. . . . I truly did have "time on my hands" and never even knew it until now, when I don't have any! Who *was* that girl who used to "moon around" (Mama's word for it!) and read so much? I feel like she was somebody else, not me, not this new me who always has something to do. Fold the diapers, feed the baby, burp the baby, put him down, peel the potatoes, pick the baby up and change him, put him in the playpen, put the water on to boil, wash off his pacifier which he has thrown down in the floor, put the potatoes in the boiling water, cut up the chicken, find the pacifier again, wash it off, etc. I won't go on and on, but you can get the general idea!

It is a major expedition whenever we go out, such as to the grocery store or to the laundromat or the library or the little playground behind the Episcopal Church up the street (St. Michael's). Or we might go to visit Susan Blankenship in #11, who has just had a baby girl named Melanie, or Marybeth Green in #45, whose John is actually three months older than Andrew, though of course Andrew is much more advanced and smarter. Andrew really enjoys visiting John. They are so cute—they love to play side by side, though they are not old enough to play together yet. This is called "parallel play"—I keep checking out all those books on child development. Sandy teases me about it, but I am just *so terrified* that I will make a mistake. Some mistakes are irrevocable, a thing I never really realized until I had a baby of my own. This thought scares me to death. I feel like everything I have ever done before means nothing, in comparison to taking care of this baby.

Sandy comes from a family of seven, so he thinks I worry too much. For instance Sandy believes in letting a baby cry, that this develops his lungs, but I can't stand it, snatching Andrew up the very minute he opens his mouth.

And let me tell you, his lungs are developing just fine anyway, thank you very much! Sandy tells me all the time that I am spoiling "that baby" but actually he is just crazy about him too, and calls him "Duke." (I'm not sure where he got that name!) "Hey, Duke," Sandy will say, and kind of box with him. They both get the biggest kick out of this little game.

So I want everybody out there to know that I am *fine*, happy as can be in this little aqua blue shoebox of a home with my baby Andrew. We are so busy in here that it is very difficult right now for me to even imagine any other world outside these four walls.

I watch Vietnam on television of course, and often think of you, Joe, but honestly it is hard for me to concentrate too long or to believe that the war is actually *real* and not just another show on television. I know that's awful, but it's true. Somehow I believe it would seem more real to me if it *wasn't* on television all the time. Honestly, my imagination has failed me on this. I'm so glad you will be home soon.

But Joe, I *do* wish you would write, at least to me. I'm sure you are hearing this from all of us, so *do* it! Make copies and send one to everybody, like I am doing here. I'm sure the Army has got a mimeograph machine *someplace*! By the way, it is hard for me to believe you scarcely know Sandy yet. Somehow I think that all the people I love, love

46

each other as much as I love them, and I forget that you all have hardly met.

Well, I will quit running on and on and tell you now about Sandy's and my first Christmas dinner together (yesterday). It was a riot! We had a baked hen which barely fit in my oven (I am *trying*, Mama!) and oyster casserole which did not work out because I used *smoked* oysters instead of the real other kind which I guess you are supposed to use. (I had bought these flat square little cans of oysters at the Piggly Wiggly, they were very expensive and blew my whole food budget for the week, but I thought you *had* to have oyster casserole on Christmas, Mama. I thought it was the law!)

Well, it *looked* okay, the cracker crumbs having formed a nice golden crust just the way they are supposed to, but the minute I bit into it, I knew something was the matter. But Sandy did not even know the difference because he had never tasted oysters before anyway. Luckily, Sandy will eat *anything*, and he thought it was delicious! We ate Christmas dinner on the floor—on our aqua shag carpet, that is!— since we don't have a table yet (though Sandy is going to build us one soon, he can build *anything*, if he can get off from work long enough to do it) while Andrew slept on his blanket right beside us. And when we got up to do the dishes, we saw it had started to snow! So we bundled poor little sleepy Andrew up in that red snowsuit you sent, Mama, and took him out in his first snowfall ever, which was coming down so thick and fast at first that we couldn't even see beyond our little row of trailers, to the street.

The streetlight made a perfect cone of light, full of whirling flakes, as we stood beneath it and stuck our tongues out to catch the flakes and tried to make Andrew stick his tongue out, too. How sweet and cold those snowflakes were, melting on our tongues, I will never forget it.

And then before we knew it, everybody from the other trailers had come out too, and we met neighbors we had never even *seen* before! such as a crazy old lady named Miss Pike, who wears the most makeup you have ever seen and used to teach singing lessons, opera I believe, and a fat little man named Leonard Dodd who described himself as an "inventor" (though I don't know what he invents), and another man named Gerald Ruffin who looked very aristocratic, but wore a plaid robe and red velvet bedroom shoes and was drunk as a lord. Somebody whispered that he used to be a lawyer but had fallen on hard times. He was in politics, too. He is from one of the most prominent families in the state. I guess he must be the black sheep of *that* family! We all talked about the snow, and passed around some of the fudge you sent, Mama, and then the Teeter sisters had us in for coffee. You have never seen as much junk as they have squeezed into their trailer—they call it "brick-a-brack." It covers every surface that is not already covered by a doily. All their coffee cups were made of flowery bone china, with gold rims. Gerald Ruffin's hands were shaking so much that his cup rattled on his saucer like a castanet. Well, I could go on and on. . . . (No doubt this is the same impulse which used to lead me to write *The Small Review*!). Anyway, I don't know whether it was that coffee or pure excitement, but I couldn't sleep a wink all night long. I lay snuggled up to Sandy like a spoon in a drawer and listened to Andrew make his snuffly little sounds in sleep, and peeped out the porthole window at my portion of the sky, which was full of whirling flakes, no two alike in the universe, and thought about my baby, and my husband, and Daddy, and all of you, and my heart was full to bursting.

Merry Christmas and love from your very poor but very happy,

Mary Copeland

P.S. I will *spare* you my recipe for oyster casserole! Oh, I also made up a big batch of Sticks and Stones for Sandy to give his boss. They were a big hit. So if Sandy gets that raise he's hoping for, it will be all thanks to me, his *wife*, MARY COPELAND!

Lee Smith

Dec. 23, 1970

*To My Dear Family and All Our Good
Friends at Greenacres Park,*

There's so much going on and so many people I want
to tell that I'm making Xerox copies of this letter.

I just can't believe that this is the last Christmas we will
spend here! In fact, this is the very *last week* we will spend
here—we are scheduled to move into our new home at
1508 Rosemary Street on Dec. 29th.

Actually, our "new" house is old, having been built in
the 1920s, but I just love it, with big square rooms and
crown molding, a beautiful cherry wood banister going up
to the second floor, and three fireplaces with fancy mantel-
pieces. I must admit it is in pretty bad shape at the present
time, needing a lot of paint and some plumbing work, not
to mention a new porch and a new kitchen, but since this is
how we got it, I don't mind. See, the landlord was advertis-
ing it as a "fixer-upper," and since I am married to a "fixer-
upper," I answered the ad myself and struck a deal. A *great*
deal, I might add! We will be living rent free in exchange
for Sandy's services, and the landlord is paying for materi-
als, of course. So 1971 will find us all the way across town,
it's almost like being out in the country.

The Christmas Letters

We will need the space, since (as most of you already know) I am pregnant with *twins*, can you believe it? They will be born in mid-February, I am hoping for Valentine's Day. I thought I was getting awfully big, awfully fast, but I never, ever, thought of *twins!* until the doctor told us. (And *now* Mama says that actually she had little twin sisters herself, up in West Virginia, she just "forgot to mention" that they were twins. One of them died young and the other is our Aunt Margaret.) Anyway, twins do run in the family, for sure.

And so we will be getting a ready-made family real fast! We could never stay in this trailer after the twins are born—we just wouldn't fit—but in a lot of ways, I hate to leave. We have been so happy here. Sandy says I am crazy, but I swear I will even miss all this AQUA—can you believe it?

Most especially I will miss all of you, and want to take this opportunity to say so. Miss Pike, thanks so much for keeping Andrew for me whenever I got into some kind of a *bind*, which you know I am prone to do! and for teaching him the little songs on the piano, that was very sweet. Ditto to the Teeter sisters, I am sorry about the teapot and the Japanese porcelain lady. Thanks to you, Mr. Dodd, for expanding my mind. (I will never forget what you told me about how you invent things: "First," you said, "I imagine a need . . .") GOOD LUCK, Mr. Dodd. Don't forget to close your door and lock it when you go out, ditto your car when you park it, now what will you do without me?

Lee Smith

Susan and Marybeth, let's make a pledge that we will always stay in touch our whole lives long, and have reunions when we are old and rich and these little babies are taking care of *us*! I will never forget that heat wave last summer when the babies played in the plastic pool every day while we sat under the sprinkler in the shade to keep cool.

And what would I have ever done without *you*, Gerald Ruffin, and your insomnia which equals mine, especially during that same heat wave. . . . Oh, how many nights did we sit out on those lawn chairs talking the night away? while the bugs circled the light bulb and my nightgown stuck to my back in the awful heat! And even this fall, with the twins waking me up all night long kicking, I didn't even mind so much, knowing you would be out there smoking, ready to keep me company. It has been a real education, Gerald Ruffin, and I thank you for it!

Speaking of education, I think it is great that you're going to finish college early, Ruthie! We are all real proud of you, especially your nephew Andrew who calls you "Roofie" ever since he knocked out his front teeth. He looked exactly like a pumpkin at Halloween, it was the cutest thing, I wish you could have seen him! with that hair even redder than Sandy's.

Joe, I have mailed a big thing of Sticks and Stones to you early, I thought you could share them with everybody else in the hospital. I sent you several other presents, too, I just hope they will arrive in time for Christmas. Let me know. Mama says she prays for you every day and I do too, my version of this being that I *think* about you every day, and all the games we used to play and all the things we did as children. I only hope my own children will enjoy each other as much as we did, and love each other as much as we did. Please write, Joe. One thing in your package is a writing tablet and a whole bunch of envelopes already stamped and addressed to me at our new house.

We look forward to Mama's visit when the twins arrive. This will be especially good for Andrew, I'm sure, who is likely to get his nose out of joint because he has gotten all the attention around here for such a long time—close to four years now! Sandy said he would get him a dog to make up for it, but Andrew now says he wants a kitten. Well, Sandy is just *not a cat person*, plus he thinks everybody should have a *dog*, and he is real strongminded, so I don't know what will happen. . . . Families! You wonder how any of us survive them, don't you? But we do.

I just wish you could all see our funny little silver tree with its blinking lights this Christmas, surrounded by presents and packing boxes stacked to the ceiling all around, not to mention *us* crammed in here tight as a drum, with me just pushing this big stomach around. Actually Sandy bought this little artificial tree because he says they are a better bargain, and I wept that he had bought a *silver* one instead of green, but I must say it *is* pretty. Andrew stands in front of it by the hour, entranced by these blinking lights. This is a Christmas we will never forget, that's for sure!

> *Love,*
> *Andy, Sandy, Mary, and the*
> *Twins-in-Waiting Copeland*

P.S. I have finally convinced Mama to share her recipe for

TACO SALAD FROM BIRDIE'S LUNCH

1 lb. ground beef, browned and drained
2 bunches green onions
1 8-oz. bottle Catalina dressing
1 diced tomato
2 c. rotini noodles, cooked and drained
1 pkg. taco mix

Add taco mix and Catalina dressing to beef, mixing well. Add all other ingredients, mixing well. Serve over plenty of shredded lettuce, with taco chips on the side.

The Christmas Letters

Merry Christmas from the Copelands, 1975!

(Especially to Susan and Marybeth, and all my good friends on Rosemary Street—I miss you so much already! Especially Elaine and Edie, remember all those crazy diets we tried? I guess I will just have to stay fat now.)

I write to you from our brand new home at 38 Hummingbird Heights, built by Copeland Construction of course! (Just like this Xeroxed letter also comes courtesy of Sandy's company Xerox.) It is a split-level brick contemporary with four bedrooms and a big back yard with lots of room for the children to play. In fact our yard serves as the playground for the entire neighborhood, which is fine by me. I love to have company while watching the kids, and all the kids love to play on the huge wood-and-tire climbing thing which Sandy built for them. (Actually he designed it and then sent Randy and Tim over here to build it for us—thanks, Randy and Tim! It's a big hit!)

The twins have turned out to be little tomboys—absolutely fearless—they scare me to death. This very minute, as I write, both Melanie and Claire are hanging upside down from the "monkey bars"—I can't even look! Andrew is inside doing an art project for school. At 8½, he is already quite an artist. In Cub Scouts, he and Sandy made a Pine Box Derby race car which was a statewide winner, and Sandy claimed that he didn't have a thing to do with it. He says it was Andy's design entirely. All Andy's teachers have remarked about his talent, I know he didn't get it from me!

I didn't even try to pick out paint colors or wallpaper for this house, for instance, I just left the whole thing up to Sandy, he has a much better eye than I do. I can't even hang pictures on the wall, according to him! He says I hang them too high. So Sandy has done it all, and I must say, everything has gone much more smoothly as a result. And this house really does look *great*! In fact it looks so good, it often seems to me that it must be *somebody else's* house. . . .

Oh, I guess I was just attached to that old "fixer-upper" on Rosemary Street, and to the trailer before that, if you can imagine! Sandy says I am "hopeless," and I guess I am! It is a good thing that *somebody* in this family is so modern and forward-looking.

I remain very busy with "the here-and-now." Little James is already learning to walk, and I can tell that he is going to be a holy terror before long. (I feel like every baby I have gets wilder and wilder—more active, at any rate. Especially as compared with Andrew, who was so *good*. . . .) But Sandy gets a kick out of James, saying that he is "all boy," which is certainly true.

We took the whole family to Halfmoon Island for two weeks again this summer, and really enjoyed it, though

Sandy left after a few days of course, he just had to get back on the job! (He is building 9 more houses here on Hummingbird Heights, all of them in the $75,000 range.) But Mama and Ruthie and I got to catch up on everything, and all the kids got along beautifully, they practically lived in the water. We had great weather the whole time.

After several job changes, Ruthie is now in the sportswear business in Atlanta, working as a "girl Friday" for a young entrepreneur named Jay Moretz who has started his own line of leisure wear which you may have seen in the stores, named "Saturdays." Their logo is a little red sailboat, I know you have seen them.

When I asked Ruthie *exactly* what she does, she said she "makes Jay Moretz possible"! (In my own way, I could identify with that.) Anyway, Ruthie is just as crazy as ever, still a "firecracker," as Daddy used to say, bless his heart.

We were having this conversation while sitting out at the beach under a pink striped umbrella on the prettiest day of the summer, all bright blue and yellow, a day to break your heart. (Now why did I say that? I sound just like Gerald Ruffin!) Anyway, the waves were rushing in and the sun was shining on them in a way that really did make them look like they were "dancing," and the air was so clear, not that kind of haze you sometimes get in summer, but clear as glass, I felt like I could see all the way to

England where I have always wanted to go. All my children were in view—the twins, running out and back endlessly, chased by the waves and then chasing them, squealing and squealing—James, asleep for once, on the blanket beside me in the umbrella's pink shade—and Andrew alone up the beach a ways, poking in the sand with a stick and staring out at the horizon, thinking deep thoughts, which he is (probably unfortunately) prone to. Mama sat in a beach chair beside me while Ruthie lay stretched out flat in the sunshine a few feet away, covered with baby oil and iodine, wet cotton balls on her eyelids, tanning herself scientifically with the kitchen timer. She turned over every 20 minutes. Sandy had gone back up to the cottage to make a phone call but now he was coming back down the dune, kicking sand like a boy. From where I was, he looked like a boy, and Ruthie still looked like a teenager. I, by contrast, felt *old*, though I am not but 31, of course. The twins were squealing and squealing, the sun glinted off the waves, and for a moment I felt breathless, don't you remember this, Mama? You asked me if I was all right. Then Sandy came and ducked back under the umbrella and sat down beside me and lit a cigarette and squeezed my knee and I really *was* all right again. It was only for a moment that I had thought, *Oh Lord! Who* are *all these people*?

Now I hope you will not think I am too crazy, reading

that last paragraph, because I *do* love everybody so much, and I am so proud of Sandy—our life really *is* the American Dream come true! Of course Sandy works all the time while I am busy running after the kids and driving carpools and keeping the books for Copeland Construction Company, but I must say I *enjoy* this job, as it is just me and Sandy up way late into the night sometimes, just the two of us, trying to make it all balance out . . . once we sent out for a pizza at 1 A.M.!

Also I am still teaching Sunday School at our church, following in Mama's footsteps once again, I guess (just like the Christmas Letters), though now we have become Methodists (Sandy's choice) instead of Church of Christ. The Methodist Church is right down the street from us here in Hummingbird Heights, so Sandy thought it would help us all get adjusted faster to our new lifestyle, and honestly, one church is as good as another as far as I'm concerned! The First Methodist Church has a very active MYF, so the kids will like it better anyway. The singing is not as good, I must say, but I love the prayers and responsive readings in the back of the Hymnal, which are just pure poetry in my opinion. That may not sound very religious, but it is true!

Anyway, as you can tell, life is full and good—maybe it is *too full*, but it is still good. We only regret that it did not work out for Joe at Copeland Construction, but we wish you good luck, Joe, in whatever field you decide to go into. This goes for everybody—here's to a happy and productive 1976!

> *Lots of love to all of you*
> *from all of us,*
> *Sandy, Andrew, Claire,*
> *Melanie, and James and*
> *Mary Copeland*
> *(Wow! What a mouthful!)*

And speaking of "mouthfuls," here's an indispensable recipe from *Cooks on the Run*:

SPEEDY ITALIAN SUPPER

1 lb. sweet Italian sausage
1 lb. hot Italian sausage
A couple of peppers & onions
1 lb. pasta, any kind
1 large jar spaghetti sauce

Cut up sausages and sauté with vegetables. Add spaghetti sauce, heat through. Serve over pasta.

The Christmas Letters

*Merry Christmas! to Ruthie, Mama, and
Close Friends Only,*

Now that Copeland Construction is sending out those
big metallic cards—I did not pick them out, in case you get
one of those too! Back to the old carbon paper for this letter.
I'll try to type hard.

And let me say that it is a *relief* to sit down for a minute! I am surrounded by boxes as I write. This is getting
to be an old story, isn't it? I don't know why we never seem
to move in the summertime, it would be so much easier.
But I have told Sandy, this is *it*! I plan to *die* in this house!
You should have seen the way he looked at me when I said
it. Then he just about died himself, laughing at me. Of
course a man does not relate to a house the way a woman
does—for Sandy, a house is something you *build*, not something you *live in*. And I'll swear, he can't even look at a
piece of land (or a mountain, or a beach) without imagining
a house on it. Or *something* on it . . . and now they are building golf courses, too, as I have mentioned before.

This house, which I hope to die in—so write it down in
your Rolodexes—is #5 Stonebridge Club Estates. It's a

"new" Victorian with so many turrets and terraces that I
lose track of them. Sandy and the decorator had a "field
day" planning everything. It's a lot of fun, but almost too
grand for me! I feel like somebody on a British show on
public television, as in "Upstairs, Downstairs."

You know that I have been after Sandy for years to *slow
down*, relax, get a hobby . . . well, the good news is that he
has taken up golf—he says that if he's going to build these
courses, he might as well learn the game. The bad news is
that he's gotten so "hooked" on it that he spends every free
minute out on the course, it's like another job! *Men!* But I
guess he is enjoying it—poor thing, he deserves to, he has
worked so hard all his life, you know, even in junior high
and high school down in Florida. Sandy never wants to
talk about his past. He says he has "put all that behind"
him. Which is certainly true—why, we barely *know* Sandy's
family. His parents have been dead for years, and I have
never even met two of his brothers, who live out West. I
think this is a shame, but Sandy says it is American! It
certainly isn't Southern, as I pointed out to him, but then
Florida certainly isn't the South.

Oh well! Who am I to say? I had it so easy, by comparison. And as for the kids today, well . . . " 'nuff said"! We
give them too much, if you ask me. I think they *all* ought to
work. But strangely enough, Sandy disagrees with me on
this, he is just so proud that they don't *have* to! He wants

them to concentrate on extracurricular activities so they can get into real good schools. So that's what they are doing.

This means that I am in the car constantly, driving everybody everywhere to clubs, practices, etc. As I told Sandy recently, sometimes I feel like I am *part* of the car, like a fancy gearshift or something. But I guess it will be worth it. James is already a state-ranked Junior tennis star at 11. This past year, he has had matches in Greensboro, Wilmington, Kinston, you name it. And those matches *last forever*, let me tell you. Actually I am privately not even sure that they are good for kids, what with John McEnroe as a role model! They throw their rackets and everything, often (it seems) encouraged by their parents, who are just as competitive as they are. I am proud to add that James never does this. He has beautiful manners on the court, his coach insists on it. Sandy thinks tennis is good preparation for life, but I am not so sure. Anyway it is a big relief for me now that we have moved so close to the club, so James can just walk over there for his lessons. It will also be convenient for Claire and Melanie next summer, as they are both on the swim team.

At school, however, they go off in opposite directions. Claire is the cheerleader and math whiz, while Melanie is very active with the drama club and literary magazine. I'll swear, it's like each of them represents a different side of the brain! (I guess Claire must take after *you*, Ruthie!) I have never seen so much energy, or so much talking on the phone. Actually, this goes for *both* of them. We have had to put in a separate phone line for the twins. They remain best friends despite their different interests, though it's easy to tell them apart now that Claire has cut her hair and Melanie has let hers grow so long. I'll be glad when they can get their driver's licenses —or I *think* I will. It will certainly be easier for me, but of course I will never know exactly where they are then. . . . Well, there are things you can't afford to think about too much, as a mother. The whole world is so dangerous, isn't it? and yet we have to let them go. Somehow it is harder to let girls go than boys, Sandy feels this way too, I know it is a sexist attitude on our part.

Andrew has already been accepted at an art school in Boston, after winning the Danziger Art Award last May when he was only a junior. Even I am forced to admit that all those years of a messy room (read, creative kid) have really added up to something special. I will actually *miss the mess*!

Sandy has always expected the boys to enter Copeland Construction Company with him, but it looks like he will just have to wait for "James McEnroe Jr." to come along, since Andrew clearly marches to a different drummer. Andrew didn't even tell us that he had applied for early admission to art school! In a way, Andrew is just as independent and bull-headed as his dad, I guess this is why they have clashed so much over the years. Of course Sandy is just as proud of him now as I am. I confess, I can't seem to get it through my head that Andrew is actually graduating! It seems like just yesterday to me that I was walking him to first grade at the old Cobb School, when we lived on Rosemary Street. I remember how tight he held my hand.

Ruthie and Jay have finally produced their first child, Eliza—Ruthie says her biological alarm clock finally went off! Now she acts like she invented motherhood. (Just kidding, Ruthie!) Seriously, she has also developed a new line of maternity clothes called Mother Nature. Look for them in stores everywhere, starting next summer. Personally, I think this is a great idea, remembering all those awful plaid overblouses we used to wear back in the old days, with *bows* and things . . . where *does* the time go? Now the idea is to let your belly show, Ruthie says it's much more natural. Some of the Mother Nature dresses are actually *knits*!

Mama is fine, in fact she's amazing, still running her little restaurant. Of course she is heartbroken over Joe's disappearance, as am I. Sorry to interject a note of sadness into the Christmas letter, but I want to ask all of you to let me or Mama know *immediately* if you hear from him, or if you spot him anywhere. (Randy Billings, one of Sandy's foremen, swore he saw Joe on the street in Chattanooga, Tenn., but this lead did not pan out either.)

Sandy and I have now joined a couples gourmet club which is a lot of fun. The other couples are John and Dovie

Birmingham, Hap and Sarah Swann, Brenda and Roger Raines, Mary Lib and Bo Clark, and Sam and Ruth Wingate, many of them neighbors here at Stonebridge Club Estates. Each couple is responsible for dinner once a year (we meet every two months). So far we have had a Hibachi Grill-Out, a Northern Italian Evening, a Mexican event, and an English High Tea—Sandy nearly starved! It will be our turn in May. Any ideas? Maybe I should just bring Mama over here to cook for everybody—Sandy is really "into" gourmet, but I still think there is nothing like Mama's home cooking. This reminds me of something funny Mama said the last time she came for a visit. I had taken her and the girls to an early morning swim meet, picking up some coffee and bagels on the way. Mama didn't say a thing when I bought the food, but the funniest look came over her face when she bit into her bagel. "Well!" she said. "Whoever thinks this is good has clearly never tasted a biscuit!"

What else? I continue to volunteer at the PTA Thrift Shop and the Altar Guild (I have given up the Sunday School class) and recently I joined a women's book group— I decided it was time to take "time for myself." I am really enjoying it.

> *. . . And to all a good night,*
> *Mary*

P.S. From the files of the Gourmet Club (these are really good)

RUMAKI
(Chicken Livers with Water Chestnuts)

6 chicken livers (about ½ lb.), each cut into 3 pieces

6 canned water chestnuts, drained, each cut into 3
pieces

9 slices bacon, cut in half lengths and partially
cooked

6 scallions, cut in 1-in. pieces

Marinade:

¼ cup soy sauce

¼ cup dry sherry

1 tsp. brown sugar

2 Tbsp. sesame oil (optional)

1 slice fresh ginger root, 1 inch in diameter, ¼ in.
thick (or) ½ tsp. powdered ginger

Combine soy sauce, sherry, brown sugar, and
sesame oil in non-metallic container. Squeeze in
fresh ginger root with garlic press. With sharp
knife, cut a small incision in each piece of chicken
liver and insert a piece of water chestnut. Place pre-
pared chicken livers, precooked bacon slices, and
scallion strips into marinade. Mix well to coat, and
let stand for at least one hour, longer if possible.
Drain, reserving marinade.

Wrap a bacon strip around each piece of
chicken liver with water chestnut. Secure firmly
with small well-soaked bamboo skewer. On 9-inch
bamboo skewers place 3 wrapped chicken livers,
alternating with scallion slices. Lay on platter and
pour reserved marinade over all.

Place on oiled grill over medium coals for 5 or
6 minutes, turning to crisp bacon evenly. Serve
each skewer on individual plate with small fork.
These should be served *hot*!

(Contributed by John and Dovie Birmingham)

Dec. 10, 1989

To my dear family and friends,

It's early for me to be writing the Christmas Letter, but
there's so much to say, it may take you until Christmas to
read this one. Mama died peacefully in her sleep this past
August, at age 67. She had no illness, or symptoms of any
sort, beyond the slight "slowing down" you would expect.
She was as mentally sharp as ever, right up to the day of
her death. The last person to talk with her, her next-door
neighbor, Mrs. Muncey, said Mama was fussing about
where the paperboy had thrown her paper—up in the

shrubbery by the porch where it was hard to get to, instead of the yard. Mama always read the paper, and always watched the news. She was a remarkable woman.

It's funny—I can't say I actually had a *presentiment*, but that Sunday right before her death, I suddenly dropped everything and got in the car and took off to see her. I can't say why—I just *felt* like it. Sandy thought I'd gone crazy, of course, but it was the Member-Guest Invitational at the club, and I knew he would never miss me. I knew he'd be over there all weekend anyway.

It was a hot day with a white sky that seemed to blend in with the fields on the horizon. The road ahead of me was shimmering in the heat, the way it does in summer. There's never any traffic on 111 South—my kids used to call it the "ghost road"—so I got there in no time. I found Mama walking around the house in her black and white voile dress and her stocking feet, just home from church. I stood outside the screen door for a minute and watched her. She opened first one drawer, then another. She peered all along the top of the mantel, then felt behind all the books in the bookcase, those old *Reader's Digest Condensed* books which she had had ever since I could remember. She reached up to touch the top of the grandfather clock.

"Surprise, Mama!" I said from the door.

"Why, hello, Mary." But Mama did not seem at all surprised. She smiled her old sweet smile at me and gave me a big hug when I stepped inside. I did not point out that she had left the door unlatched—we were always trying to get her to lock it. Though she had been losing weight for a year or more, she seemed strong as ever when she hugged me. Then she held me out at arm's length and looked at me good, her blue eyes starred by the cataracts which the doctor said weren't "ripe" enough to operate on.

"How's the kids?" she asked, and I said, "Fine."

"How's Sandy?"

"Fine."

Then she asked, "Heard from Joe lately?" and I said, "Mama, you know I haven't heard from Joe. I would have called you if I had."

"Well . . ." Mama said. She kind of let it trail off. "I was just thinking that you might have heard from him," she said. She was looking at me with her head cocked to the side like a bird. It was the first time she had mentioned Joe in I don't know how long. Then she slapped her thighs in that familiar getting-down-to-business gesture. "It's a good thing you came up here today," she announced. "I can *use* you, Miss Mary!" and before I knew it, she had stuck an apron on me and had set me to cutting up green tomatoes and onions at the same old white enamel kitchen table I remember so well from childhood.

"How come we're making so much of this pickle relish?" I thought to ask when I'd been chopping for almost an hour. Mama looked at me darkly from the stove, where she was stirring up the first batch. "Why, Mary," she said, "you know perfectly well that Mr. Hughes won't eat a thing without it!" So that was that. Mr. Ray Hughes, who runs Hughes Hardware Store across from the courthouse, had been coming to Birdie's Lunch every day for 20 years.

We sweltered all afternoon in that hot kitchen, breathing in pickles until our eyes watered. Of course Sandy had insisted upon air-conditioning Mama's house years before, but Mama refused to turn it on, claiming that air-conditioning was bad for her arthritis, a medical notion she had gotten from *Parade* magazine. We cooked while it got darker and darker outside, then windy, as a thunderstorm came up all of a sudden out of nowhere, rolling in across the fields from the coast. We cooked while the air grew heavy and the light failed, and thunder crashed over our heads, and lightning branched across the sky. Then the rain fell hard for ten minutes, pounding on the roof. In an instant I was transported back to the world of my childhood on the farm, when Joe and I used to huddle under an old blanket on the porch glider during thunderstorms, caught up in delicious fright, telling each other long, complicated stories that scared us both to death. I kept on chopping tomatoes.

After a while I looked up to see Mama smiling at me. "You're cutting them up too big, honey," she said, and I started cutting smaller. I don't know where the afternoon went. Before I realized it, we were done, the jars in a glistening row on the windowsill, the green tomato pickles glowing from within, like jewels. I kissed Mama good-bye but paused in the doorway to look back and see her searching those bookshelves again—for what? I will never know. There is so much that we can never know.

I headed north on the "ghost road" toward Raleigh with a warm, full heart. I imagined Mama getting ready for prayer meeting, exchanging her house slippers for those old black lace-up shoes that the twins called her "witch shoes," powdering her face with the same loose powder she had used since time immemorial, Lord knows where she still bought it, and driving that old green Buick over to church as she had done twice every Sunday for so many years, through a long succession of preachers whose names I could never remember (she had taken to calling the most recent one, Mr. Trimble, "that nice little boy-preacher").

The next day she went to the dime store as usual. She fed some of the new pickle relish to Mr. Ray Hughes, who was heard to pronounce it "damn fine." Then she came home from the store, complained about the newspaper to Mrs. Muncey, watched—I am sure—the news and "Major Dad" on TV, and went to bed. I'm also sure she said, "Now I lay me down to sleep, I pray the Lord my soul to keep," as she always did when putting Joe and me to bed. I do not say this prayer myself, nor have I taught it to any of my children. I don't know why not, actually. But now this strikes me as awful. I have always envied Mama her faith, and now I envy it more than ever, as I struggle to go on without her. I keep forgetting she's dead—whenever something happens, I automatically reach for the phone to tell her about it. I guess I will go on doing this for a while.

Sandy says I should consider it a blessing in disguise, as Birdie's Lunch was due to be closed this coming spring along with the dime store, a new Wal-Mart out on the highway having put them out of business. James Grady had been running the store at a loss for the past two years—mainly, I suspect, to give Mama something to do. He was just about as fond of her as we are. *Were.* As we were.

Anyway, it is hard to imagine how we will face Christmas without her, since she always made the gravy for the hen, and brought the Sticks and Stones and pound cake with her. I have already made the pound cake and the Sticks and Stones, but I don't know how I will make the gravy. I never could make gravy worth a damn. I believe it is a lost art among my generation!

But on a happier note, we have had lots of other changes in the Copeland household, too. The biggest news is that I have gone back to school. I have always had a secret dream of doing this, have long held this possibility in the back of my mind. And all of a sudden, after Mama died, I just did it! I drove across town and registered at the

McKimmon Center for Continuing Education at N.C. State. Technically I am classified as a special student. But if all goes well, I will become a regular student, starting second semester. This thrills me beyond belief. I guess I have realized that we don't live forever, and that the only time to do what we really want to do is *now*. This is the thing about a parent's death—especially the *second* parent's death— suddenly there is no other person standing between you and the great beyond, that darkness, the grave. I know I sound morbid, but it has been such an illuminating insight for me that I have to share it with you. Listen: *the time is now. We are the next in line.*

I guess you think I am being pretty dramatic when all I've actually done is sign up for a few classes! But to me this is a *big deal*. My stomach was actually turning flip-flops when I turned in my first paper. I was terrified! My humanities professor is a young man named Dr. Winters, from up North. (I can just hear Mama now—"that little boy-teacher," she would have called him!) He is a thin, moody, intense young man not much older than my Andrew, very smart, and he is a *Marxist*! I have never met one before. It is quite interesting in class, because everything we read, we have to look at the economics and the politics of the time. Dr. Winters believes that any book is primarily a product of its time. I am not used to thinking of things this way, and at first I just bit my tongue, but now I feel free to argue with Dr.

Winters, who actually seems to *like* it when people disagree with him!

My other class is Narrative and Expository Writing, and here I am having a "field day." My teacher is an old fat rumpled fellow past retirement, Dr. Rutledge, who seems "out of it" much of the time yet occasionally fixes us with his bleary old eye and says something I know I will never forget, something I have to write down in my notebook and mull over for days, like I used to do with Gerald Ruffin. Dr. Rutledge has been extremely encouraging about my writing, as well. All this writing (we have to do weekly compositions, with revisions) has taken me right back to myself as a child, to Joe and me and those *Small Review*s we used to sell in the neighborhood, to myself and how much I used to love to read and write. It's like a string that was broken has been re-tied, or re-attached—suddenly I feel a sense of continuity between that child I once was and the woman I am now. I did not realize how completely I had been cut off from her, and for how long. Obviously I will major in English, as I started out doing so long ago, but I will have to struggle through the other courses too, of course. I'm sure it won't hurt me a bit! Though I have never felt so ignorant.

One of my first assignments in my composition class was to write about a *process*, so I wrote about how to take out a stain. It was the only "process" I could think of. And I can get a stain out of anything, as Sandy will tell you! Hair spray removes a ballpoint-ink stain, for instance. Put meat tenderizer on fresh bloodstains, and salt on red wine stains. White vinegar and water for pet urine. Mr. Rutledge was simply astonished. He gave me an A, commenting upon both my writing and my "esoteric area of expertise." (I had to look up "esoteric.")

Well, I don't mean to blither on, but all this has been enormously exciting for me. Also it is so easy to "blither on" now that Sandy has gotten me this new computer and printer (which will make me as many copies as I ask it to!), an early Christmas present. (Sandy has been very supportive of my going back to school, once he got used to the idea. At first he couldn't believe I was serious.) The kids seem real proud, too. In fact, if all goes well, son James might be starting out at N.C. State about the same time I finish (too bad he can't major in girls!). The other kids are fine, and so are we all.

Love,
Mary Copeland

MAMA'S GREEN TOMATO PICKLE RELISH

½ peck green tomatoes (20)
2 stalks celery
10 green peppers
24 large white onions
2 large cabbages

8 pounds brown sugar
3 tablespoons whole cloves
16 tablespoons mustard
2 teaspoons cinnamon
½ teaspoon red pepper

The Christmas Letters

1 cup salt   8 tablespoons ginger
3½ quarts white vinegar

> Pare tomatoes and chop fine; cut stem from green peppers, remove seeds, and chop fine; shred the cabbage; chop onions and celery fine.
>
> Mix ingredients. Add salt and let stand 1 hour. Drain. Make a syrup of vinegar, brown sugar, and spices. Scald the syrup, add the chopped mixture, and simmer, after it has been brought to boiling, for forty minutes. Yield 8 pints.

Feb. 6, 1991

To our dear family and friends,

First let me apologize for the lack of a Christmas letter from the Copelands this year! I *know* this has never happened before, but listen:

I've got some good news, and I've got some bad news.

The bad news is that Sandy had to have a triple bypass on December 15th.

The good news is that the surgery was completely successful and he is *just fine*, so he is very lucky—we are *all* very lucky!

The most alarming thing about this is that Sandy felt perfectly okay, exhibiting *no symptoms at all*. And you know he has always kept his weight down, as opposed to Yours Truly. Anyway, what happened was that Sandy had to go to Duke University for a complete physical as required for insurance purposes. (Johnny Cook, Sandy's partner in the new developments down at the coast, insisted that the company take out this huge policy on him.)

Well, things were going great until the stress test. They took him off the bike and sent him straight to a hospital room —wouldn't even let him come back home for one minute! I had to pack his things and take them to the hospital for him. (Of course I took all the wrong things, I was so rattled. . . .) They did an angioplasty the next morning, and operated two days later. Sandy was *fit to be tied*, of course! Not that it mattered. You know how those doctors at Duke are. (This is why we didn't come to any Christmas parties, in case anybody was wondering. Mystery solved! Sandy wouldn't let me tell anybody except the kids until it was all over.)

But he has been a model patient ever since, and now we are both involved in this very arduous program they recommend. (Actually they do *more* than recommend— they tell you flat out that you have to change your lifestyle if you want to stay alive!) So we are both doing all of it— the diet, the walking, etc. I'm sure it is good for me, too. Every other day we go over to the Life Center so they can monitor Sandy and we can be in a support group. Honestly, it's just like AA! Naturally, Sandy *hates* this part, he's so private, and feels that people ought to keep their own worries and concerns to themselves. He says he doesn't want to hear about anybody else's life! not to mention sharing his own. You know how men are—no wonder they have the most heart attacks. But I'm learning a lot, let me tell you. Also Sandy bemoans so much time spent "just walking," as he puts it. (At first he was carrying his cellular phone, but the doctor took it away from him.)

Naturally Christmas was somewhat disorganized this year, as you can imagine, but I had done some cooking ahead, of course, and the twins pitched in with the rest. I am not even ashamed to say that we had a delicious smoked turkey from the Catering Company! And we certainly had a lot to be thankful for on this holiday.

What else? Here's a quick rundown on the kids. Our budding poet Melanie loves the academic world and is planning for graduate school, while Claire is already an intern at Carolina Telecom, a company I have yet to understand the true nature of! Andrew continues to pursue his art career on the West Coast—he couldn't make it for Christmas this year as he was "hanging a new show" in San Francisco and also moving from San Francisco to L.A., which sounds like a terrifying place to me, but which Andrew apparently loves. He has rented a little studio house up in the hills near that HOLLYWOOD sign, you know the one I mean. Anyway, all the kids are fine, and I guess I am, too, though I had to take Incompletes in all my courses and now am killing myself trying to finish them up, plus take the two I had enrolled in for *this* semester. I may have to drop one of those, actually.

If I can just make it through the semester, we have a wonderful summer vacation planned (Sandy is being forced to take vacations now, hurrah!) to Scotland, where he will golf and go to fly-fishing school (a new hobby which is supposed to slow him down) while I curl up in some ancient place reading long English novels to my heart's content.

Happy Valentine's Day,
Mary Copeland

Appropriately enough, I send along our recipe for

❤ ORANGE-MINT SHERBET ❤

4 cups orange juice
¼ c. chopped mint

Blend and freeze in ice cream freezer.

The Christmas Letters

Merry Xmas! to Ruthie and good friends—

1992 will find all the Copelands busier than ever, heading off in a million different directions. Those hard years with Sandy and me working all day long, and then poring over the books together at night, seem almost like a dream to me now. And speaking of dreams, Sandy and I had a real "dream vacation" in Scotland, though I feel like I have scarcely seen him since, he has been so busy putting in "Plantation," Copeland Construction's new multi-million-dollar coastal "village" and golf complex. They are paying special attention to the environment, trying not to disturb the fragile ecology of the marsh or diminish the wild charm of the island itself. So Sandy has been down at the coast a lot, while I have been struggling with chemistry and *loving* Twentieth Century Lit., especially a seminar on "Images of Women" that I took this past semester. I plan to do my Senior Thesis on Virginia Woolf.

I also took an extremely interesting and challenging American Studies course this past semester. One day I was in the library doing research on "The Sixties" when another person from the same class, a young woman, turned to me and said, "Why, Mary, I'm surprised to find you here. You were *right there* during the Sixties, weren't you? I shouldn't think you'd need to do research."

"Listen," I told her, the truth coming to me even as I spoke, "I was *alive*, if that's what you mean. But I missed the Sixties entirely, as a matter of fact. I was just too busy having babies and Tupperware parties."

She stared at me blankly for a moment before she shrugged and went back to her microfilm. She didn't get it.

But *you* get it, right? You know what I meant.

I must admit that virtually all my assumptions have been seriously challenged in these past two years—I highly recommend going back to school for anyone who wants to have a more open mind! I have come to actually *like* Melanie's tattoo now, for instance (a vine around her ankle)! And I've decided it's definitely a good thing for young couples to live together before taking the (drastic) step of marriage—although I can just imagine what Mama would have had to say about that! We are very fond of Melanie's friend Bruce, a musician, and (once we got used the age difference) of Claire's young lawyer, who is raising his two children by himself, apparently. (Can you *imagine*? He seems to be doing a pretty good job, too.)

Everybody will be coming home for Christmas, including Andrew who is bringing a friend from California. And I've got to finish one late lab report before I can even begin to cook! Though we may be "ships that pass in the night," you have to admit we're heading off in some interesting directions!

> *Love and Peace,*
> *Mary*

Tuesday, Dec. 10, 1993

To Ruthie and My Very Special Friends,

A *REAL* CHRISTMAS LETTER, THE FIRST EVER

First, my apologies for not writing a Christmas letter last year (for not returning calls, for not returning letters, etc.). The fact is, for a long time I couldn't do anything. Not a damn thing. Nothing. I was shell-shocked, immobilized. This was followed by a period when I did *too many things.* Marybeth, who has been through it, wrote to me about this time, saying, "Don't make any big decisions"—very good advice, and I wish I'd followed it. Instead, I agreed to a separation agreement, then to a quick no-fault divorce, then to Sandy's plan of selling the house P.D.Q. I just wanted everything *over with*—the way you feel that sudden irresistible urge to clean out your closet sometimes.

Listen: if this ever happens to you, resist that urge. *Go slowly.* I didn't even get a lawyer. Sandy and I used the same lawyer, at his suggestion. Now I know how dumb I was! Well, I don't intend to go into that part of it. But the point is, I actually trusted Sandy—and why not? I had trusted him all these years.

I kept smiling and smiling, and signing things. Everyone remarked upon how well I was "taking it." I just kept on smiling. After smiling for three or four weeks I stepped on the scale one day and was amazed to see that I'd lost 20 pounds without even realizing it—that 20 pounds I've always been meaning to lose.

I was really in bad shape. Every month after Sandy left, in fact, I'd look back and think, *Oh, I didn't even know what I was doing then. I was in such bad shape! Look how much better I am now.* But then another month would go by, and I'd look back at myself again and think, *Well, I really didn't know how crazy I was a month ago! Lord, I was crazy then. But I'm so much better now.* And then another month would go by, and . . . well, you get the picture. It has taken me a long, long time. And I'm still not there. I'm still not "adjusted." I don't think I will ever be "adjusted"! I don't even know what this means anymore. I remember thinking (as I cleaned out the house and stuck everything into Village Self Storage, fueled by that crazy manic energy that comes with divorce) that I wished I could just put myself in there as well, to emerge after 5 or 6 years like Rip Van Winkle, miraculously "adjusted," having avoided all the pain which I am still going through.

The Christmas Letters

I didn't actually realize that the marriage was over, oddly enough (not when we signed the papers, not when we went to court —none of that really registered) until I walked through our empty house for the very last time right after the closing. As I left the lawyer's office that afternoon and got in my car (Sandy got in *his* car, of course) I noticed that my house key was still on my key ring. Without stopping to think, I drove straight over there. I hadn't been back for months, not since renting this nice little place in Oakwood.

Real estate agents don't waste any time—they had already hung a SOLD banner across the FOR SALE sign. It was April, and my bulbs were in bloom—all the daffodils in back, the crocuses by the mailbox, the tulips in their raised beds along the terrace. I had grouped them by color, and they looked like a proud little army on parade. The windows shone like diamonds—I guess they'd just been cleaned, for the new owners. I didn't know anything about the arrangements for selling the house. Sandy had taken care of all that, as he had always taken care of everything. *Why, he could have cheated me blind,* I realized, though of course I knew he *wouldn't*—Sandy was always very scrupulous about money (as opposed to his private life, more later on *that!*)

For the first time, I wondered why I hadn't insisted on being more involved, why I had been so happy to have things done for me, decided for me—so happy to relinquish control. Anyway, the house looked great. The trim had been touched up, the terraces had been pressure-washed, the lawn service had obviously just been there.

I unlocked the front door and opened it. It swung inward silently, giving onto the gleaming wood floor of the entrance hall, *like the shining path in the Wizard of Oz,* I thought briefly, crazily, and then I was walking the house, going into each room. It's a huge house, of course, I'd forgotten how big it is. An afternoon hush had fallen everywhere, so that my heels clicked and echoed as I walked from room to room. The rooms are large and airy, beautifully proportioned. Sunlight streamed in the big windows and French doors, blinding me.

There was not even a trace of us left. None of the family snapshots stuck up on the refrigerator with magnets; none of the terra-cotta pots that had held my spice garden on the kitchen windowsill; none of James's tennis rackets which used to hang on the wall of his room; none of Andrew's endless collections of stamps, of bird books, flower books, constellations; none of the twins' endless array of old coats and jackets in the hall closet where they'd been accumulating for years . . . all I could see was what had been. I walked through the whole house slowly, then returned to the gleaming foyer to stand for a moment just before I left for the last time, and that's when it really hit me.

This is the end, I thought. *This really is the end of us as a family, the end of my world as I have known it, the end of me as*

the person I have been since I first met Sandy. That's when I
started to cry. I cried and cried—loud, choking sobs, like
a person who has lost everything, which I had. (But in
another way I hadn't, of course, though it would take even
more time for me to know this.) I suppose it was only fit-
ting that I should face the end of our marriage there, in the
last of our houses, and I thought of them all—the trailer at
Greenacres Park; that wonderful old place on Rosemary
Street, with the tin roof; Hummingbird Heights, with the
great yard and the fantastic jungle gym, always full of tum-
bling kids, all of them grown and gone now; and then
finally this "castle," as Melanie used to call it, Stonebridge
Club Estates, the last one, the last shell ever to hold that
family which we once were.

Well, I cried and cried.

But after about thirty minutes of this, a funny thing
started happening. Imperceptibly, even in the midst of all the
crying, I felt my spirits start to lift. This continued. I could
actually feel energy coming into me, some essential energy
that seemed oddly familiar, like an old friend you don't quite
recognize at first. Now, I believe—without dramatizing too
much, I hope!—that this was the moment when my *self* came
back, or when I came back to my own real self again.

I found some Kleenex in my purse, blew my nose,
dropped my key on the floor in the middle of the hall, and
opened the door. The lock clicked shut behind me, and that

was that. Sunlight was everywhere, so harsh against my eyes, but I didn't care. I got back into my car and drove around the circle and down the long driveway, and did not look back. I have not looked back since.

Until today, I suppose, when I decided to write a Christmas letter again. Why not? I've got a lot to say. And the Christmas letter was always *my* thing, not Sandy's, though for so many years of course I signed both names, and thought of us as one.

Thursday, Dec. 12, 1993

Two days have passed since I began this letter. Two extraordinary days in which I drove over to Village Self Storage and got out the copies I kept of all my Christmas letters from former years. It was so dark in the storage unit that I could scarcely see, and despaired of ever finding anything, but luckily they were right there at the entrance in Mama's old hope chest from West Virginia, next to a box of Andrew's drawings and another box labeled "Trophy Collection"— God knows what all is in that storage unit! Now I begin to wonder if this is healthy or unhealthy, under the circumstances, to save so much. Oh who knows?! I have had it with shrinks and marriage counselors, of which more later.

The Christmas Letters

At any rate, I found the letters easily. I brought the chest back here (along with two boxes marked CHRISTMAS ORN., I figure I might as well make a little effort this year, though I certainly don't have "the Christmas spirit"), made a big pot of tea for myself, and started back at the beginning, reading. 1967 through 1991. Twenty-four Christmas letters, 24 years of family life stuffed into these envelopes and stuck away just as easily as Sandy has stuck me back into "the past" already, that dark box into which he has consigned so much: his childhood, his family. . . . Well, *I* just can't do it! I'll have to haul everything out eventually, I'll have to go through it all again, "healthy" or not—

Several things have struck me, reading back through all the years.

We really were "in love," Sandy and me. We really were a family. It was all true. No matter what Sandy says now or what he said in the midst of his mid-life crisis following the heart surgery, or what he said later during our so-called "marriage counseling" (ha!) sessions, we really were *together* in every way, for many years. Those years count too. The story told in my Christmas letters is a true story. It is the story of our marriage.

Of course there are other stories too, stories *not* told in those letters, and they are equally true. Back in Greenacres Park, for instance, there was the story of how scared I was, alone with a new baby all day long, how he had colic and would not quit crying and would not quit crying until I thought I would go crazy, until one day I started shaking his crib I got so mad, and then I sank down on the floor and started crying, scared to death, afraid I had hurt my baby. Which I had not. But that story is true too, as true as the story of how much I loved him, and loved taking care of him and Sandy in those early days. See what I just wrote? *Taking care. Taking care of Andrew, taking care of Sandy.* Isn't that interesting? A person reading back through these letters might decide that my life has been largely a function of other people's lives, and that would be true too, or at least it would not be untrue. There is one letter in which I almost came to this conclusion myself, back in 1975, but I could not stand to know it then, and pulled back from the realization. Well, why not? Though true, it wasn't the whole story either.

During my recent "shrinkage" I have learned all about "denial" of course, but really it seems to me that denial is often a good and useful thing, keeping us going, allowing us to do what has to be done in the world.

Another story I didn't write at Greenacres Park was the story of Gerald Ruffin, that charming brilliant alcoholic Gerald Ruffin who loved me (and he really *did* love me, probably as much as Sandy and more than anybody else ever will love me again), and how we used to sit out on those crummy lawn chairs talking and talking all night

long sometimes while I patted Andrew's back as he lay
facedown on my lap and mewed like a cat from colic, while
the bugs flew around and the BIG AL'S TIRE sign shone all
night long just beyond the blooming honeysuckle that covered the stockade fence enclosing us from the "bad neighborhood" which surrounded us on every side. Oh, how
sweet that honeysuckle smelled—I will never forget it.
And Gerald Ruffin's profile, outlined against the sign's red
glow . . . well, he was simply the handsomest man I have
ever seen. He looked (oh, I don't know) *English*, I thought,
with that fine aquiline nose, the chiseled chin, nothing
weak about it though he *was* weak, poor thing, he couldn't
bear his vision of the world. Oh, Gerald Ruffin had a story
too, of course, and it was a tragic one, involving a brother's
betrayal and a child's death by drowning and his young
wife's suicide, years before. Gerald Ruffin was 41 years old
when I met him. I was 22. I thought he was ancient, of
course, but now that I'm older than he was then, I realize
he wasn't ancient at all, and I can understand how a person
such as he might take to drink.

Gerald Ruffin had been living in Greenacres Park for
several years when we moved there, and I believe I was the
only person he had ever really talked to in all that time.
Once a week, a dignified black man wearing a porkpie hat
would arrive at Gerald's trailer, sent by his brother, and
deposit two paper bags full of groceries on the stoop by

the door, tip his hat to me if I was outside with Andrew or standing in my own doorway, and then disappear, and sometime during that day the groceries would disappear too. Not that Gerald Ruffin ever ate much, growing thinner and thinner before my eyes.

In fact I never saw him eat *anything*, and I never saw him without a drink in his hand. He drank from a silver julep cup, a remnant of better days. He drank vodka and vodka only—Stolichnaya—he called it his "one extravagance." Whenever he ran out of vodka, he'd call a cab (he'd lost his driver's license years before) and jump right into it, sometimes still wearing his bathrobe, and have the cabbie drive him to the liquor store and then go in to make his purchase for him, while Gerald sat in the cab magisterially surveying the world outside Greenacres Park "which certainly does not have much to offer," he'd announce grandly upon his return.

Did I ever sleep with him? No. Did I ever kiss him? Oh yes, Lord yes, many many times in the dead of night with the overpowering smell of that honeysuckle all around us and my own hard-working Sandy asleep inside the trailer. I kissed him in the daytime too, and people saw it—I know Mrs. Pike saw us at least once, but she never said a word about it, I guess she was old enough and wise enough to know what was important and what was not.

The Christmas Letters

I was a good wife. And I was a good mom, too. I got
the hang of it. I was also a desperately lonely unhappy girl
who might not have made it through those first two years
of my marriage without Gerald Ruffin's conversation
("palaver," he called it, a word I have never heard anybody
else use) or those sweet, sweet vodka-flavored kisses, all
the sweeter for their hopelessness. This is why I don't drink
vodka now, by the way. I have never been able to taste the
stuff since without the memory of Gerald Ruffin springing
straight to mind, which always makes me cry. I am crying
now. They say that vodka has no taste, but this isn't true. You
can taste it. I can taste his kisses still, all those years ago.

Which is one reason I got so upset when that marriage
therapist urged us to "put all our cards out on the table"
and talk about "any infidelities." Sandy came up with
plenty, of course. Over a dozen. Over a dozen women
("girls," he called them) he'd slept with while he was married to me! But they were "not important," he said. Just
girls he ran into while "out of town" or "at conventions,"
or "sales meetings," where he was "lonely," so it "didn't
count." (Dovie Birmingham *did* count—more on that!)
Anyway, the point is that Sandy had all these affairs to put
out on the table, so to speak, while I had not one infidelity
to report, not one.

I could have kicked myself for not sleeping with

Gerald Ruffin, who loved me, I know he did. Perhaps I could have rehabilitated him, saved him, married him . . . certainly, I would have learned a thing or two!

Oh, but that would be another story, wouldn't it? Another story altogether. Gerald Ruffin died of cirrhosis of the liver in the VA Hospital in Durham in 1979, while we were living at Hummingbird Estates. I kept up with him all that time, calling every week, visiting every month. He weighed 85 pounds when he died. I never mentioned these visits to Sandy, who probably wouldn't have remembered Gerald anyway. It was another story.

As is the story of my brother Joe, a real tragedy. Joe never should have gone to Vietnam. He never should have gone to *any* war, he was not cut out for it. *I* could have gone to Vietnam more easily than Joe. I have always been able to pull myself together to do what needs to be done, but this was not true of Joe. Joe was so sensitive, so imaginative, *fragile* really, though he kept this side of himself success-fully hidden from most people. The fact that he was good at working on cars and engines made him seem like he was stronger and tougher than he was—you know the connota-tions, the connections we all make between cars and men, between men and war.

Well, Joe was not even really a man, not yet—he was just a boy, and not even a very tough boy. (In later years, I would see so much of Joe in my own Andrew, though of course Joe was not gay. Or: I don't think Joe was gay. But who knows? He didn't have a chance to be much of anything, I guess, before we lost him.)

And we *did* lose him in that war, as surely as if he had been killed.

This was the awful tragedy of it, Joe-who-was-not-Joe coming back, Joe who looked exactly like the old Joe (the curly black hair, the one-sided grin, the snaggletooth) and laughed like the old Joe, and walked like the old Joe, that easy shamble, but was all hollow around the gray eyes which had gone flat and distant somehow, eyes which could no longer quite focus on whoever he was with. And he couldn't pay attention either. He'd be talking to you, and then he'd simply stop talking, and stand staring at a point somewhere just beyond your face. And then he'd walk away.

This is what happened when Sandy tried to give him a job at the construction company. The first day on the job, Joe'd be great, firm handshakes all around, joking with the guys. And he'd outwork them all—he could build anything, put anything together. He'd be whistling, Sandy said. Enjoying himself. Joe was always a great whistler. Then the second day, or maybe the third or the fourth, he'd just walk off the job. Leave for lunch and never come back. Take a cigarette break and bye-bye.

He'd be gone for a day or two, then show up at Mama's

or back at our house, all smiles, whistling, glad to see everybody. So then Sandy would try to talk to him, and give him another job with another crew, and before you knew it, the same thing would happen all over again. Sandy knocked himself out to no avail. I have never seen him so frustrated. Sandy always *liked* Joe (well, Joe was so likable, wasn't he?) even though he never really knew him until after Vietnam. And I think perhaps Sandy felt guilty himself because *he* never had to go, because we had a baby. But Mama felt guiltier than anybody, and talked about it constantly, assuming all the blame, which was wrong, of course. If anybody was to blame it was Daddy, who never could see more than one side to anything. Right or wrong, black or white. Mama was fond of saying that Daddy had "the courage of his convictions." But is this strength of character, or is it stupidity? Now I wonder.

I remember that time Daddy hit Joe when we were kids, the day of the flood, when he was whipping Ruthie, and Joe tried to stop him. (Isn't it funny how some things will stick in your mind forever while others, more important or so you'd imagine, simply disappear?) I remember that Joe had on a green International Harvester cap, that he nearly fell down the front steps, that his feet made a sucking noise in the mud as he stumbled away.

I also remember, as if it were yesterday, one of those discussions they had (Mama, Daddy, and Joe) about what

Joe would do if he got drafted. Sandy and I had driven over from Raleigh shortly after our marriage. I was in the first trimester of my pregnancy, and couldn't keep anything on my stomach. So in addition to being sick, I was really nervous, for I knew that my elopement had broken their hearts, no matter what a brave front Mama was trying to display at the time. It was already cold, sometime after Halloween. I remember how the dead stalks of corn stood up in the fields, how the sky was all red and silver. I have always liked winter sunsets the best. Sandy had to pull over twice to let me throw up. But then finally we were there, driving slowly through town just as the streetlights came on, past the dime store (closed, it was Sunday).

We pulled up in front of the house. Sandy opened my door and took my hand and kissed me once, hard, before I turned the glass doorknob and stepped inside. This was the third time I had been home since my marriage. The first time was awful—Mama cried, Daddy stalked upstairs, and Joe tried in vain to hide his disappointment. The second visit had been strained but cordial. Joe was not at home.

So I was praying that this visit might be better—we had come to pick up a loveseat and a rocking chair that Mama had offered us in a gesture of what I hoped was reconciliation.

And as soon as we walked into the kitchen, I knew it would be all right. For I was no longer the problem.

Joe was the problem now. He and Daddy sat facing each other across the old white enameled kitchen table where Mama did all her cooking (this table I have now in my own kitchen in my own little house). Both of them were smoking. Cigarette smoke hung blue in the air above the white table, beneath the hanging globe of the lamp. Mama was at the sink, back turned, tension evident in the way she stood. Daddy and Joe were staring at each other. They looked exactly alike: handsome, angular men with long faces and those wide expressive mouths.

"No son of mine . . ." Daddy began.

"Hi, everybody," I said, and Mama whirled around to hug me with her hands still wet, the first real hug I'd had from her since our marriage, and I was so glad to get it.

"Honey!" she exclaimed. "How are you feeling? Did you all get any dinner?" she asked Sandy, who allowed as how we had not, since I hadn't felt up to eating, and then Mama was feeding us cold fried chicken, and they were telling us everything.

Daddy was trying to get Joe to enlist, believing that this would give him "more choice" than if he waited around to get drafted. Sandy immediately agreed (I believe this is the very minute that Daddy decided he was okay) and recommended the Marines. Joe sat there like a rock looking so miserable that at last I took pity on him and said, "Why not the Navy? I think their uniforms are the cutest," which made everybody laugh, it was such a silly remark in the middle of this serious conversation. (Here is another thing that I have always been good at, playing a little dumb in order to make everyone laugh, to relax a room.) Joe grinned at me but remained uncharacteristically silent in the center of that conversation which whirled and eddied all about him, a rock in the midst of the current. Sandy ate three or four pieces of chicken and praised it extravagantly. He and Daddy were deep into a discussion about what the government ought to do about draft dodgers when Joe slipped away.

It was the first time I ever remember him slipping away like that, and it was the last time Sandy and I were to see him before I had my baby and Joe was drafted.

Only of course we didn't know any of that then. I just thought, Oh well, Joe's gone over to the shop to work on a car and listen to music (his favorite occupation). I didn't really think anything about it at the time. I was just happy that Daddy was finally talking to Sandy (I always *knew* they would get along if they'd give each other a chance) and that Mama seemed glad to see me.

And in fact, the worst was over. Right as we were getting in the car to leave, she gave me a whole set of dishes that she'd gotten for me with Green Stamps, saying, "Well now, just go ahead and take these with you. I was going to give them to you for Christmas, but I can't wait." Which was typical of Mama!

Daddy knew it, too. "Aw, shoot, Birdie. Now you'll just have to get her another damn Christmas present," he said from the dark front porch. All I could see of him was the red tip end of his cigarette in the dark. "You all be careful now," he yelled as we drove off.

So Mama blamed herself for what happened to Joe. She couldn't blame Daddy, as he was dead, and anyway she had sanctified him in her memory as he never was in life, where he had been a stubborn opinionated hard-working man like most others of his time and place, no better and no worse. Oh, how I had loved him myself, for his faults as well as his virtues! (I guess it is easier to love a father than a husband in this way.) In any case, Mama never got over it, just as Joe never got over it. "If only I had stood up to your Daddy!" she'd say later. Or, "If only Joe had gone to college!" etc. But it was too late. (Sometimes it can be too late, sometimes things are irrevocable.)

And you know what I think Mama was looking for, that very last time I saw her? I think she was still looking for some clue as to what had become of Joe, searching in the only places she could search, the little familiar nooks and crannies of the life he once had shared with them but then could share no longer. Or perhaps Mama was remembering all those endless detective games which Joe and I had played as children, especially the Hardy Boys games, when I was Frank and he was Joe, of course.

The Christmas Letters

And now I am Mary Pickett again, having resumed my maiden name. I did this yesterday, at the courthouse downtown. It's a very simple procedure. I'm not sure exactly why I chose to do this, since I am still "holding on" to all those things in my storage unit. But clearly, the name change has something to do with reading through these old Christmas letters. For one thing, I was fascinated to note how many different ways I'd signed my name over the years—there are all these different names at the ends of the letters. So I have decided to have only one name from now on: *Mary Pickett*, though I suspect I will always see the "Copeland" there too in my mind's eye, my ghost name, just as Nov. 2nd will always be my ghost anniversary.

Another fascinating thing about the Christmas letters is all the recipes—I feel as if I have written out my life story in recipes! The Cool Whip and mushroom soup years, the hibachi and fondue period, then the quiche and crêpes phase, and now it's these salsa years. I have spent my entire life cooking and (Lord help me!) putting the leftovers into smaller and smaller containers.

That brings up the Gourmet Club, so I guess I'd better get the business of Dovie Birmingham over with right now.

As far as I was concerned, it all began at Dovie and John's anniversary party in the summer of 1988. It was billed as a "pool party," designed to inaugurate their new swimming pool as well as celebrate their twenty years of marriage. I didn't even take a bathing suit, of course, as I had no intention of showing my body to everybody in town, especially to all those people you see in other contexts, such as your dentist or pediatrician, for instance. And sure enough, it was a *huge* party. All the members of the Gourmet Club were present, of course, plus lots of other neighbors from Stonebridge Estates, members of John Birmingham's law firm, and their many other friends. The Birminghams had a wide circle of acquaintance due to his civic interests and her vivaciousness. (This was the word everybody used whenever Dovie Birmingham's name came up: "vivacious.") In fact, Dovie was a small energetic woman with too-large breasts that almost seemed to tip her over, like Dolly Parton, short thin fluffy white-blond hair and pale eyes that always darted around a room, assessing the situation, seeing how she was doing. I don't mean to be too hard on her here. In fact I always liked Dovie Birmingham just fine until that very night, the night of her anniversary party where I was only trying to be helpful, in a neighborly way, by volunteering to go out to their new pool house and get some ice from the deep freeze since they were running low at the bar inside and at that moment our hosts were nowhere to be seen.

Have I mentioned that the Birminghams' party featured a Hawaiian motif? It also featured blue drinks that looked like Windex, with little umbrellas in them, and leis

for the ladies, though so many ladies had come that they'd
run out of leis early on. I had not gotten one. I wore a long
loose flowered dress which looked vaguely Hawaiian, I
hoped, though I'd bought it in the lingerie section of Dil-
lard's that afternoon. Getting into the spirit of the party, I'd
taken off my shoes at the door, and I can still recall exactly
how the damp grainy pebbled concrete of the patio felt to
my bare feet as I walked out to the pool house, examining
the Birminghams' new pool which I found almost ostentatious, actually, since it was so big and the country club was
practically next door anyway. It was an irregularly shaped
pool with that pebbly concrete (plus lots of plants and fake
"rocks") laid out in such a way as to make it all look "natural," though it was not natural, of course, no more natural
than the plastic lily pads floating on the water. A little artificial waterfall trickled endlessly into the pool, making rip-
ples. No one was swimming yet.

The pool house was supposed to look like a pagoda. I
went around the back and pulled the door open and there
was my own husband Sandy kissing Dovie Birmingham
who immediately began to squeal like a stuck pig. She was
holding one foot up in the air like a teenager in one of those
old *Beach Blanket Bingo* movies. In fact they *both* looked like
people caught in a still shot from a Grade B movie, standing there beneath the humming fluorescent lights of the
pool house.

"Mary?" Sandy said.

"Oh shit," Dovie Birmingham said. She had a smudge of red lipstick all over one of her big front teeth.

"Excuse me," I said, shutting the door. I was terribly embarrassed, and felt somehow guilty, as if it were all my fault. I walked back around the pool carefully, noticing the interesting dark blotchy shadows on the bottom created by those plastic lily pads. The pool *was* ostentatious, I decided. Still barefooted, I walked straight through the party and out the front door of the Birminghams' house and two blocks through the neighborhood to my own house, where I surprised Melanie and two of her friends smoking marijuana in the portico. Normally this would have "thrown me for a loop." But I didn't even mention it. I merely said I had a headache and went upstairs and lay down, soon to be followed by my ashen and contrite Sandy, carrying my shoes in his hand, full of apology and explanation. He said it had never happened before, that he didn't know what had come over him, or *them*, actually—he didn't know what had gotten into them, though he blamed himself, of course. Dovie Birmingham was not in any way to blame. Sandy had had too much to drink, that's all. It would never happen again, that was for damn sure! Damn sure!

"Now come over here, honey," he said, "and forgive this bad old man."

Well, I did.

The Christmas Letters

And if you are surprised by that, then you don't have a *clue* about who I was during all those years. Of course I forgave him. I was dying to forgive him, feeling, as I said, that it was my fault anyhow. I decided I had gotten too wrapped up in the kids, had neglected the marriage. (Now I believe that whenever you start thinking about "the marriage" like it's a needy third person, you're in trouble anyway.)

So Sandy and I "made up." We "worked it out."

This lasted for about ten days, until John Birmingham paid a call on us one evening right after supper. I remember that he telephoned first. Sandy and I went to the front door and watched him walk straight across our yard, right through our underground sprinkler system like he didn't even notice all the sprinklers going at once, and I don't believe he did notice them. Clearly, here was a man with something on his mind. Once inside, John Birmingham refused to sit down, and got right to the point.

"Sandy," he said, "Dovie tells me that you and she are in love, and that you plan to get married. She says this has been going on for over a year."

John Birmingham is an aging preppie who went to Carolina for both his undergraduate and law degrees, and looks like it. This was not supposed to happen in his life. He did not even so much as glance at me. Nor did my husband.

105

"Mary," Sandy said, "why don't you go check on the children, honey?"

Which was exactly what I had been thinking. But they were all gone at that moment—mercifully, thankfully— James playing tennis at the club, the girls off Lord know where, and Andrew away at school, of course. After I made sure that the house was empty, I came back down the stairs to find the entrance hall empty too, except for a little puddle of water where John Birmingham had been standing. The door to the study was closed, and remained closed for over an hour. I waited there uncertainly for a while, and then went back to the kitchen and washed the dishes and listened to NPR. (This is what we do, isn't it? We listen to NPR while the whole world crashes down around our ears, it's the only thing we can think of to do.) Finally I heard the front door close, and then Sandy came into the kitchen and stood behind me and put his hands on my shoulders.

"John was mistaken," he said.

"But Sandy—" I started crying.

"John was mistaken," Sandy said again, "and that's the end of it."

Only it wasn't, of course. Dovie Birmingham immediately moved back to Dallas, where she was from, taking their only child, a little girl ("one of those puny late-life babies," Mama had said once, about this child), with her. John moved into an apartment and put their house on the market. At first it was priced too high, and didn't sell. I kept tabs on this, for some reason, driving past it at least twice a day. Once, during this period, I stopped my car on impulse, got out and entered the Birminghams' back yard through the side gate, and went out to stand by the pool. It was September, but hot. I had been to a bridal luncheon at the club. All of a sudden I stripped down to my underwear and jumped into the pool. It felt great! I swam a number of laps and then treaded water for a long time, enjoying the musical sound of the little fountain. The ends of my fingers had gotten all wrinkled up by the time I got out and went home.

You know most of the rest of the story.

A year later, Mama died and I went back to college. Then Sandy had the heart operation. Now I believe that "the marriage" never recovered from this operation. It was as if "the marriage" had had its own heart attack, and died on the spot. Sandy and I were still alive, of course, never more fit and healthy due to that follow-up program at the Life Center. This is also when we first went to the marriage counselor (never go to a "marriage counselor," just get a divorce!).

Our marriage counselor, whom I hate, is named Peter Waterford, a mellow little guy with a goatee he loves to finger. (I saw him just the other day, in traffic, driving a new Lexus. I know we paid for that Lexus, so I certainly hope he's enjoying it!) Anyway, at the marriage counselor's urging, we went to Scotland, a nice trip which staved off the inevitable. Sandy played golf, I read. We both enjoyed ourselves. (It was somewhat like "parallel play," which I mentioned in one of my very first Christmas letters when Andrew was a baby.) We avoided all serious discussions, all dangerous topics, as if they were water hazards on one of those gorgeous Scottish golf courses. Then we came back from Scotland and threw ourselves into our work: I, into my senior thesis; Sandy, into "Plantation," his development down on the coast.

Though we were necessarily apart a good bit that year, I remained hopeful. In fact we both remained hopeful, I believe, and endlessly solicitous of each other, conducting nightly telephone conversations whenever we were apart ("How was your day?"—"Fine, dear, how was *your* day?" etc.) like nurses who keep on giving artificial respiration to a patient who has died.

This phase lasted until that girl's mother called from down at the coast, looking for her. Her grandfather had had a stroke, and she should come home immediately. "She's not here," I kept saying, though the woman insisted, politely, that she was. "Isn't that funny?" she said before she hung up. "I've got the name written down right here."

I hung up and telephoned Sandy in Wilmington, where I got his answering machine. I could have stopped right there, never mentioning the incident to Sandy, but I did not. I could not. This time I had to push forward, to know. It gets pretty trite and sordid from here on out. I confronted him; he lied to me; I just couldn't believe him, though I wanted to—oh, how I wanted to!

We went back to the marriage counselor, Peter Waterford, for that session I will never forget. We were all sitting around a gleaming mahogany table, kind of a conference table, in Peter Waterford's lovely office way up in a high-rise building which overlooked north Raleigh. I could see I-40 and the Crabtree Valley Mall, far below. Peter Waterford made a little tent of his fingers, leaned back in his chair, and looked at us in a gentle shrink-like way.

"I think it's time to put all the cards out on the table," he said. "Honesty may be painful at first, but it is ultimately healing, creative."

"What do you mean?" I asked. I looked at Sandy.

Sandy knew exactly what he meant. Sandy kept running his hand through his thinning red hair, sort of patting his scalp, in an odd gesture I had never seen before.

"Sandy?" Peter Waterford pressed.

"You mean you want me to come right out and—"

"Yes," Peter Waterford said ever so gently.

This is when Sandy told me that he had slept with over a dozen women who "didn't count," plus Dovie Birmingham, who did.

I seized upon this phrase. "What do you mean, 'don't count'?" It drove me wild.

"Oh, Mary, they didn't mean anything to me, I've always loved you, you know that. I still love you. These were just girls at conventions, like that meeting I have to go to in Houston every year. You know it gets real old, real fast, being in a hotel room by yourself. . . ." Sandy went on and on, once he got started, pouring out a whole litany of transgressions which I can't really remember now because it was just at that point that my mind began to wander. I can't account for this, but it is true. I was trying to pay attention, I really was, but I kept thinking about other things, other times.

Sandy talked for a long time, and then finally he stopped talking.

I sat there.

"*Mary,*" Peter Waterford said.

"What?" I said.

Peter Waterford is one of those people who says your name too much, I suppose he thinks it establishes intimacy or something. "Mary, in spite of his obvious pain and embarrassment, Sandy has been totally honest with you. He wants to make a clean sweep of the past, Mary. He wants to establish a brand new relationship with you. He wants to begin again, Mary."

I sat there. I was thinking about a time years and years ago when Joe and I were little, making Easter baskets in the dime store with Mama and Daddy and all the women who worked there. I have no idea why this particular day came so vividly into my mind at that moment.

"It's time to put all your cards out on the table now, Mary," Peter Waterford was saying.

I shook my head, unable to speak.

Sandy was staring at me.

"Just play the hand you've got, Mary," Peter Waterford said.

Suddenly the whole card-game metaphor struck me as unbelievable, a ridiculous way for grown-up people to act.

I grinned at them both. "I fold," I said.

Sandy lurched forward in his chair. "Mary," he started.

I stood up. "I'm not playing this game anymore," I said, and left before either of them could stop me. Having never actually slept with poor Gerald Ruffin, I had nothing to put out on the table anyway, but I wasn't about to admit it. Anyway, I was sure—I *am* sure—that there was more love, more concern and care and feeling, in my relationship with Gerald Ruffin than in all of Sandy's affairs put together. This is the truth. It is my story, and it is true, too. Lots of things are true: that I loved Sandy with all my heart and gave him my pretty years, that he loved me as well, that I am the only person in the whole world who knows or ever will know many things about him, large and small, such as that he runs down his shoes in the back and does not ever read books and is terrified of cats and will buy that horrible chocolate cereal and eat it if left in a house by himself. I know he cried all night when Andrew told us he was gay but since that time has done his very best to adjust to it, going so far as to blow up at Johnny Cook who once asked Sandy if he thought he'd ever be able to "forgive" Andrew. "Forgive him, *hell!*" Sandy exploded. "What are you talking about? What have I got to forgive him for?" an attitude which would surprise most people who know him. Sandy looks like a stereotype but he's not. Maybe nobody's a stereotype once you really get to know them, but this gets harder and harder the older we get, it seems to me. Too much ground to cover, too much to learn.

I'm probably a stereotype myself, come to think of it, one of those women you see on every college campus these days, those fiftyish women with half-frame reading glasses and denim skirts and Aerosole shoes, streaked hair pulled back in a ponytail, kicking along through the leaves, on fire with Woolf or whoever.

That's me.

I'm a stereotype too.

But at least I'm not a *fat* stereotype any longer, having magically dropped those 20 pounds of "divorce weight," as Marybeth calls it. I have emerged with cheekbones to die for, not that anybody cares . . . oh, that sounded bitter. I am *not* bitter, actually. I truly believe that Sandy is

doing the best he can. We all do, don't we? We do the
very best we can. We "keep on keeping on," as Mama
used to say.

In fact I am having a little group of my women friends
from school over for lunch tomorrow, just something really
simple (shrimp salad). They have been such an endless
source of support for me, as have you all.

Now I want to end this nearly endless Christmas letter
by sharing something with you. I want to tell you what
came into my mind at that moment in the marriage counselor's office, the moment when I did not put any cards on
the table, the moment before I walked out. It was a little
memory, that's all, an image from my childhood.

It is a cold dark Sunday afternoon, several weeks
before Easter. Mama and Daddy have taken Joe and me to
the dime store with them, to "help make the Easter baskets." All the women who work in the store are there too,
and lots of toys, and lots of candy. The women form themselves into an informal assembly line, laughing and gossip-
ing among themselves. They're wearing slacks and tennis
shoes. They're drinking coffee. It's almost a party atmosphere. As "helpers," Joe and I don't last long. We stuff ourselves with candy and then crawl into a big open cardboard
box of pink cellophane straw where we sleep all afternoon
while the straw shifts and settles around us, eventually
covering us entirely, so that no one can find us when it's

time to go. I wake up with Joe's warm breath in my ear, his heavy little leg thrown over mine.

"Mary!" I hear them calling. "Joe!" Their voices sound far, far away. The overhead lights in the dime store glow down pink through the cellophane straw. It is the most beautiful thing I have ever seen.

"Mary! Joe!" It's Mama, then Daddy calling. Joe makes a sleepy little noise in my ear. "Mary! Joe!" I know I have to answer them soon but I hold the moment as long as I can, me and Joe all safe and secure in our own bright world, sought by those who love us. I am thinking, *I will remember this. I will always remember this.*

I have, too. And it is my Christmas gift to you tonight, this perfect moment, as real as the psychological strip poker game in the marriage counselor's office with which it coexisted, another story, yet both of them happening and happening and happening forever at the very same time, and both of them true.

Merry Christmas.

Love,
Mary

The Christmas Letters

*Happy New Year 1995 to my
Invaluable Friends!*

After delivering myself of that interminable epistle last
year, I had decided not to write this year—a decision in
line with my decision not to "do Christmas" in a big way
either, as Sandy chose to remarry on Christmas Eve (she's
21 years younger!) and all the kids except Andrew were
involved in that. Andrew wasn't able to get here in time
due to prior commitments.

Anyway, Sandy's wedding was in that big Episcopal
Church downtown, six bridesmaids including Melanie and
Claire, the whole bit. The bride wore a long white dress,
and why not? It's her first wedding, poor thing. I rented
some good videos (*The Dead* and that wonderful Canadian
thing about the old women on the bus), then took a cold
lovely walk around the block (big stars, clouds of breath).
All the houses I passed either had a full-bore Christmas
tableau visible in the windows (family, tree) or nothing at
all—dark, locked up. I was trying to manage something in
between, which is hard here in America, I suppose. I came
home half frozen, brewed a pot of tea, and talked to some
of you on the phone.

Near midnight, just as I was turning off the lights, here
they came! "dressed to the nines" and looking wonderful.

Lee Smith

First to arrive were Melanie and her friend Bruce, Melanie in her red satin bridesmaid's dress, something she would *never* choose to wear though it was very becoming, I must say, and Bruce in a tuxedo (beyond belief, he plays in an alternative rock band named Steel Wool) though I did think Bruce could have shaved a little better. (But they like a little stubble, don't they? I guess it's "in" now.) Anyway, I really enjoyed this, as it has been years since I have seen Melanie dressed up! She always wears black. For the wedding, she had pulled all that long curly red hair up into a knot on the top of her head. She looked positively pre-Raphaelite! Of course she got back into her jeans in short order. Even though it was so late, she just couldn't wait to show me a literary magazine containing her first published poem. The magazine is named *Bitteroot* and the poem is named "Evening Light, Pawley's Island." I'm no judge, but I think it's wonderful. (It doesn't rhyme, of course.)

Then here came Claire, Don, and Don's adorable little girls, ages 8 and 5 (they remind me of you and me, Ruthie). The girls were so tired, they were practically sleepwalking. I had planned for them to sleep on the futon in my own bedroom, so Claire and Don could have some privacy. Plus, I knew I would enjoy waking up with those little girls on Christmas morning. I was struck by Claire and Don's effi-ciency, putting the girls to bed, putting out their "Santa Claus" in the living room—it's as if they have already

become an old married couple, without the honeymoon.
I feel like I'm more interested in their "romance" than
they are!

Next appeared James with *yet another* girlfriend, this
one tall and languid, from South Carolina. (New rule:
I'm not going to "get to know" each one until she's been
around at least 3 months.) But of course, she's adorable.
They're all adorable, they all fall in love with James, and I
don't blame them. He has become a very impressive young
man. I can't imagine him ever settling down—but they all
stay single a lot longer now, don't they? It seems to me that
adolescence extends to age 30 at least! (But maybe that's
better, I don't know: it's certainly true that many of our own
decisions were *disastrous*. . . .)

Anyway, we all met Adrienne, James's new girlfriend,
who turns out to be a psychologist-in-the-making, a really
interesting young woman—maybe she'll be the one. I'm
keeping my fingers crossed. (Whoops—there I go again!
Getting involved. It's hard, isn't it? Whoever thought it
would be so hard? As a child, I thought adults were, by
definition, *wiser* than we were—now I realize that they
were just *older*, and that wisdom is *not* something that will
descend upon us at a certain age, that it will not descend
upon us at all, in fact.)

Of course I was dying to ask about the wedding, but I
am proud to tell you that I *did not*, not once! The kids raided

the kitchen just as if they'd had nothing at all to eat at the reception—"Well, Mom," Claire said, "it was *hours ago*!" They downed huge Dagwood-style ham sandwiches and milk, and it was about one-thirty before we all got to bed.

Imagine my surprise when I was awakened at two A.M. by a loud banging noise downstairs. At first I was terrified. Then I heard a muffled laugh, and another banging noise— which I recognized, this time, as coming from my own kitchen—the sound of banging pots and pans. I turned on a light and checked the little girls, who had not stirred. Then I threw on a robe and stumbled downstairs.

"Hi, Mom!" Andrew stood in the kitchen door to greet me, filling it up. He gave me a good big hug. Andrew looked great, by the way—very tan, very fit. One of those new spiky haircuts.

"Mary! I'm so glad to see you!" Phil was wearing one of my old aprons.

"What in the world are you *doing*? Why don't you go back to bed?"

"*Mom . . .*" Andrew waved a box of Rice Chex in the air. "We're making the Sticks and Stones. We brought all the ingredients on the plane with us."

"You didn't!"

"Oh, but we *did*!"

I started laughing so hard I had to sit down. "You crazy things! Whatever made you think of that?"

Andrew looked indignant. "Well, Mom, *somebody*'s got to do it!"

And so we had a very merry Christmas 1994, and hope you did too.

Love,
Mary

LOW-COUNTRY BENNE COOKIES
(James's new girlfriend brought these, they're delicious)

Yield: 4 dozen cookies

> ½ cup (1 stick) butter or margarine,
>   at room temperature
> 2 c. light brown sugar
> 1 egg, well beaten
> 1 teas. vanilla extract
> 1 cup self-rising flour
> 1 cup benne seeds (sesame)

1. Cream together butter and sugar in a large bowl. Add the egg and vanilla and mix well. Add flour and benne seed, mixing well after each addition.

2. Roll dough into 6 1-inch cylinders and freeze until ready to bake.

3. Preheat oven to 325°. Line baking sheets with aluminum foil.

Lee Smith

4. Slice frozen dough thin and bake 8-10 min. Let the cookies cool thoroughly before removing them from the aluminum foil.

(From Adrienne Ravenel)

3. Letter from Melanie

The Christmas Letters

To our whole family, Bruce's and my friends, and everyone in Mom's Circle of Light,

Greetings, Blessings, and Hosannas! This is me, Melanie, getting an early start on my first Christmas Letter. Don't worry—Mom is all right. In fact she's never been better. But let me explain. Bruce and I are here house-sitting while Mom is in the Peace Corps (this way, we're saving a lot of money, so I don't have to work full-time and can write).

Since we've been house-sitting, I have noticed myself doing some interesting things: going around in Mom's old gardening shoes, for instance . . . wearing her old plaid robe . . . putting sugar in the iced tea . . . even using her little Tupperware things! Bruce can't believe it.

And today when I came across her old Christmas list, I decided it's time to write a Christmas letter. We have some big news in this family, too. Claire and Don were married last May, just before Mom left, at the Tavern on the Green in New York. We were all present, naturally—Bruce even wore a tie for the occasion. More big news is the birth of a new half-sister, Susannah North-Copeland, 7 lbs. 6 oz., in Wilmington, N. C., August 18. Dad just can't quit grinning. Andrew has a major exhibit coming up in Los Angeles in February, and James will begin Law School at Duke next fall.

Lee Smith

I've started a novel. I've been doing some research on my grandmother's family; luckily, Mom saved all of Grandma's letters, and kept up with a few cousins herself. The book is set in West Virginia, where Grandma was from, a little town named Blue Gap which has all but disappeared now. Bruce and I have driven up once, and plan to go back in the spring. The most helpful person I encountered was our cousin Miss Libba Louise Long, a maiden lady who works in the elementary school library and is always in a twitter.

I was fascinated to learn that my grandmother had younger twin sisters—one of them being Miss Libba's mother, Margaret Hodges Long, and the other being—well, Miss Libba wouldn't even speak her name! as it appears she got pregnant by an older man, a married teacher, when she was just a girl, and then died under "tragic circumstances." All this happened when Miss Libba herself was just a baby, so she never knew her young aunt at all, and now refuses to say what the "tragic circumstances" entailed—suicide? death in childbirth? accident? murder? Miss Libba Louise told me all this in a little blushing burst, then clammed up and absolutely refused to say another word about it, not even weeks later when I called.

When I looked for the page in Grandma's old Bible where she wrote down all the births and deaths in the family, her whole family tree, I found it had been torn, with the record of the twin sisters' birth mysteriously missing. Naturally I wrote to Mom right away, who wrote back to say that Libba Louise was "never quite right in the head," according to Grandma and everybody else, and that as far as Mom can remember, "that girl" died of the flu when she was about fifteen. Mom doesn't think there was anything at all mysterious about it. "That girl" was always "sickly," according to Grandma.

I'm sure I can learn her name by going through church records or courthouse records when Bruce and I go back up to Blue Gap. Maybe I can find her grave in the family "burying ground," which I haven't visited yet, since it's way up in the mountains. Another cousin has promised to take us up there, and says that he also has some of our great-aunt Rachel's papers "stuck in a drawer someplace." So I'll probably be able to come up with this girl's name and date of death, if not her tragic tale.

But since I'll never know the real story anyway, I've decided to write my own! This is basically where I got the idea for my novel, in which the whole business of twins is important, naturally. I've always wanted to write about being a twin. And though the novel is totally fiction, I've been learning as much as I can about mountain life in the early 1900s—the library here has an excellent folklife collection, which I've been poring over. So many of the customs are brand new to me—firing off guns on Christmas

Day, for instance, and celebrating "Old Christmas" on January 5th. The research is so fascinating that I have had to literally *force* myself to quit taking notes and start writing.

Every morning I put on this plaid robe of Mom's, sit down at my computer here at the old white enamel kitchen table, and gaze out the window at the birds on the birdfeeder for a while before I begin, and then begin again, and again, still trying to get it right.

Merry Christmas,
Melanie Copeland

P.S. Whoops! I almost forgot this recipe from Mom (who said not to mention the anthropologist).

NDIWOZ ZA MPIRU WOTENDERA

2 bunches fresh greens, mustard or spinach
½ teas. salt
1 bunch green onions, chopped
½ teas. black pepper
¾ c. peanut butter
½ c. water
Cooked rice

Wash and cook greens until tender. Add onions & cook briefly. Make paste of peanut butter & water, pour over greens, cook slowly for 5 minutes. Serve over rice.